A COMPLETE OVERHAUL

THE BUILDERS, BOOK 3

VANESSA GRAY BARTAL

DRY CREEK PRESS

CHAPTER 1

"Hey, Mol." Mossimo Samperi lounged in the doorway wearing *the smile,* the one that made Molly stupid.

"Hey," she said in a tentative effort to remain neutral and hold onto some shred of self-respect. Everyone thought she was pathetic because of her hopeless crush on Moss, and she agreed. What they didn't know was that he sometimes toyed with her heart, like now when he seemed to be flirting with her. Other times, coincidentally whenever his family was around, he avoided her like she was the stalker they thought she was. She poured her coffee without spilling and held out the pot to him. "Coffee?"

"Sure, thanks," he said. He remained standing in the doorway, meaning he wanted her to pour it for him like the employee she was. She set her coffee down, reached for a mug, poured it nearly to the brim, and added a generous dose of hazelnut creamer, his favorite. Moss finally eased into the room and took it from her, his fingers sliding over hers as she passed off the mug. She kind of hated him, she realized. But mostly, she loved him.

"What do you have going on tonight?" he asked as he sipped his coffee. Of course he was standing too close to her, much closer than social propriety dictated for an employer and employee. Somewhere in the back of her mind she could hear Lou Lawton saying that she could have a harassment case against him, if she ever pursued it.

"Nothing," she said reluctantly because she knew what was coming. Oh, how she wished to be able to tell him she had a date, just once. But how could she date someone else when she was hopelessly hung up on him? It was a sick circle of self-loathing he had trapped her in.

"I'm playing a gig tonight at *Truckers*. You should come and be my cheering section," he said, his warm smile lighting her from the inside.

Say no, Molly urged herself. *Tell him you can't make it.* "What time?" *Oh, Molly, you idiot.*

"Eight. Are you going to be there?" His hopeful tone was a dagger in her heart.

"I'll try," she promised, giving herself an out in case she mustered an ounce of self-control.

"You're the best," he said. His eyes fell to her lips, on purpose, she knew, before tipping his drink for a sip. He had never gone so far as to kiss her, but his warm, flirtatious glances promised things he had never acted on. "Thanks for the coffee."

"Sure," she said, watching as he drained the mug and set it in the sink, presumably for her to wash, and then left the room. Molly leaned against the counter and tried to clear her head. Why did he do this to her? Why did she let him? Because deep down, deep, *deep* down, she believed Moss was a good man. And she believed that if he ever got over his selfish immaturity, he would be the sort of man worth waiting for. Her biggest problem was that she had zero hope she would be the one to nab him, if he ever truly reformed. Most likely, she would be the dummy who put in the time waiting for him and then some other girl would swoop in and reap all the benefits.

Sighing, she finished her coffee and washed their mugs before getting back to work. The office emptied except for Benny, who remained in his office working on the company's finances in preparation for tax season. He kept Molly busy requesting files from the past quarter, and the day sped by with no further time to think about Moss. For that, Molly was supremely grateful.

But then the day was over, and it was time to leave. Molly said goodbye to Benny, drove home in her clunky sedan, and let herself into her tiny apartment. She made herself a salad and ate it at the table, refusing to sit in front of the television like a slob. Most of the life she had now was due to hard work and discipline, pulling herself up by her bootstraps alone. She couldn't afford to give in to weakness or temptation. That was why she didn't have cable. That was why she kept one credit card with a small limit and didn't allow herself to shop for anything but necessities. That was why she ate healthy and worked out. Because she was disciplined and believed in hard work. There was only one temptation Molly found too great, and his name was Mossimo Samperi.

She had spent the last three years questioning why he got to her and had yet to come up with an answer. Molly was not a stupid woman. She knew he played her. She knew he toyed with her emotions with zero intent to follow through. But she was addicted to that tiny part of her heart that couldn't stop hoping. That was why, at seven thirty, she changed from her work clothes to the clubbing clothes she had owned since high school. Her entire wardrobe was due for a refresh, but Molly was loathe to touch any of her savings on something so frivolous. She had only herself to depend on, and she needed to save for her future as much as she could. One accident, one hospitalization, one emergency or disaster, and she could be destitute and living on the street again. The security of preparation was better to her than a new pair of high boots.

She arrived at the club at exactly eight. Being punctual wasn't cool when clubbing, but Molly couldn't help herself. Being late triggered her anxiety. Moss was already on stage. He played acoustic guitar and sang lead because of course he was the type of guy who played guitar and sang lead in a band. Moss spied her and winked, and Molly felt like she might melt into a puddle on the floor.

"Hey, can I buy you a drink?"

Molly turned to see who was talking to her and came face to face with a guy who had a sweet smile. He wasn't necessarily handsome, but he looked pleasant, as if smiling came naturally.

"Thank you so much, but I'm kind of here with someone," Molly said, indicating Moss's band with a nudge of her head.

"Oh, well, take care, have a good night," he said.

"Thanks, you too," she said with a smile. Molly had encountered too many unkind people to not appreciate kindness when she saw it. She sat at the bar and ordered a cherry soda. The bartender smiled when he set it in front of her, and she dropped some money in his tip jar. She was a sucker for a smile, and she felt a little warm and loopy from so much benevolence in the atmosphere.

She faced forward and sipped her soda, listening to the mellow strains from Moss's band. They mostly played ballads, sappy covers of love songs that Molly probably wouldn't listen to in real life.

The two seats beside Molly were filled by two women who looked vaguely familiar. Molly couldn't place where she knew them from until they started talking.

"Moss is looking good," one of them said.

"When doesn't he look good?" the other one asked.

"When he doesn't call back for a month," the first said, and they both laughed.

"He's a player, for sure. Didn't you guys date kind of seriously in high school?" the second woman asked.

"We went out a few times," the first one said. At the mention of having dated Moss in high school, Molly remembered the woman's name was Colette. "I wouldn't say it was serious, though. Moss isn't serious about anything."

"I always liked Giovanni," the other girl said. Molly didn't know her name.

"For sure," Colette agreed. "He was super serious and kind of a sexy bookworm. He's married now, did you hear?"

"I know, I heard he eloped with Vivian Haslett."

"I could see that," Colette said. "Their kids are going to be total geeks."

"If they last that long. I mean, who elopes like that? Crazy. It seems like something Moss would do."

"Are you joking? Moss will never leave his mother," Colette said.

"That woman does everything for him, she does his laundry, cooks for him, pays his bills so they're not late. And she totally believes he's perfect and no woman will ever be good enough for him."

"Good thing for Moss he never sticks with anyone long enough for her to meet the mother," the unnamed girl said.

"Totally. She would never approve of anyone for her baby. Let's move closer to the stage, see if we can get his attention. Maybe he'll buy us a drink. I'm so broke my last bank statement said LOL instead of number," Colette said.

Molly sat back and watched as the two women made their way to the edge of the stage. When Moss spotted them, he called for a fifteen minute break, hopped down, and began talking to Colette. He didn't turn to look for Molly, nor come over to talk to her. She could have gone forward and spoken to him. But the fear of what might go wrong held her back because maybe he wouldn't talk to her, and what then? Could she stand the continued humiliation of losing out to another woman again? How many times had he led her on and then thrown her over for the sake of someone else? Too many to count.

She stared down into the melted dregs of her soda, clinking the ice together with her straw as she thought. Stay or go home? *Stay*, said the undying hopeful fool within her. *Go home*, said the rational portion of her, the one who had weathered her through too many storms to count. Tonight she would listen to that part of her and be glad the evening had only cost her five bucks for some soda. She slipped off the stool, headed for the exit, and that was when she saw them. Moss and Colette were at the end of a long hallway, beside a pay phone, kissing as if he were shipping off to war in the morning. They didn't notice her, and she was glad. She spun on her heel and left, trying not to sprint as she headed toward her car.

CHAPTER 2

For the next four months, Molly stayed strong. She avoided Moss, unless he needed something for work. She refused to give in to the temptation of falling for his intermittent flirtation. She had never gone so long without falling for him before, and she began to have hope that she might get over him for good.

And then they were lost in the wilderness together and nearly died.

It started the day Moss stopped by her desk on his way to a jobsite. "Hey, Mol."

"Hey," she replied, not looking up.

"What are you working on?" he asked.

"Tax stuff."

"Already? It's August. Isn't tax day like in May or something?" he asked.

"April," she replied. "But we do it every quarter, so it's sort of ongoing."

"Oh, I've never actually done my taxes," he said, trying and failing to sound sheepish.

"I know, I forward all of your W2's to your mom," she said.

"See? I don't even know what a W2 is," he said.

Molly still didn't look up. She continued to stare at her computer and type, though it was likely she was typing gibberish that would have to be redone later.

"I haven't seen you around much lately," he said.

"That new invisibility cloak was worth the money," she commented.

"Ha, yeah. It almost feels a little like you've been avoiding me," he said.

I've been trying my best. "It's been busy," she said, which was no lie. In the evenings, she did outside bookkeeping for extra income. Every little bit was a feather in her nest against poverty and certain doom.

"I've missed you," Moss said, and Molly had to fight the urge to roll her eyes. Every time she tried to put some space between them and get away, he sucked her back in again, usually with something like another invitation to come and fawn over him while he hooked up with other girls. But Molly O'Ryan wasn't half Irish for nothing. Her fighting spirit had been awakened, and she wasn't about to be bamboozled by him again.

"Is your band playing another gig and you need an audience?" she said.

"No," he drawled, either confused by or oblivious to her sarcasm. "We kind of had a fight and broke up. It happens to all the great bands at some point and, since that was our third gig and we made a total of a hundred dollars in our career together, it was completely inevitable. Someday they'll make a movie about it." He sat in the chair across from her desk and helped himself to her candy jar, reaching in for a fistful of chocolate mints. "I love these things."

I know. She knew everything about him, his preferences, his dislikes, his strengths, his weaknesses, when he got his haircut and by whom, even when he'd had his first kiss and who it was with. But knowing him wasn't getting her anywhere; it was time to move on.

"Sorry about your band," she said for lack of anything better.

"Meh, I'll find a new one." He unwrapped a piece of candy and popped it in his mouth. The action caused a few of his curls to spring free and topple over his eyes. Molly resisted the urge to push them away. He had the green eyes, olive skin, and aquiline nose of his roman ancestors. Where the mop of curly brown hair came from was anybody's guess.

She realized she was staring at him as she thought these things and jumped to attention, facing toward her computer once more. She printed a letter that needed sent out and focused on addressing the envelope.

"I think we should go out," Moss said, and Molly almost toppled out of her chair.

"What?"

"Let's have a day of fun, blow off some steam, get away from the office," he said.

What was that supposed to mean? Was he asking her on a date or a casual get together as friends? All of a sudden, she had reached her limit on ambiguity. She set down her pen and folded her hands on her desk. "Moss."

"Why does it suddenly feel like I'm about to be turned down for a bank loan?" He leaned forward and mimicked her pose, folding his hands on her desk, too. "Yes, Ms. O'Ryan."

"Are you asking me on a date?"

"Maybe," he said, smiling coyly and using his lone dimple to full effect.

She crooked her finger at him. "Come here." He leaned closer, and so did she, until they were mere inches apart. She closed the gap until they were practically nose to nose and pressed her palms to his cheeks.

"Mossimo Samperi, I have put up with a lot from you over the last three years, too much. But I swear to you that if you don't give me a straight answer this minute, I will crush you like a June bug on a screen door."

"This is so hot," Moss said. He would have kissed her, but she let him go and sat back. He sat back with a smile. "It's a fine line, Molly. You're my secretary. If anyone in my family knew I was doing this, they would kill me. If you leave the company because we tried something and it didn't work out, I'd be totally screwed."

"What do you want me to do, sign a waiver saying I won't quit if you break my heart?" she said.

"Could you?" he asked.

She opened her drawer. "I can never find my letter opener when I need to jab someone."

"Easy there, Stabby McGee. I guess what I'm saying is that I want to do a kind of trial run to see where it goes. And if we agree it doesn't work, we go back to the way it was."

"Not back to the way it was," she said. "I can't keep doing the thing where I moon over you, hoping for some scrap of affection."

"Why not? I thought it was working nicely," he said, and she tossed an eraser at him.

"If it doesn't work, we'll go back to being friends, just friends," she said.

"Deal. But Molly," he leaned forward over her desk again and took her face in his hands. "I really, really think it's going to work." His lips gently brushed hers with each word. Not a kiss, but the kind of caress intended to leave her yearning for more, which it did. "I'll see you." He let go of her face and, with a wave, walked out the door.

"I kind of hate him," Molly muttered, glad she was alone in the office for the rest of the day.

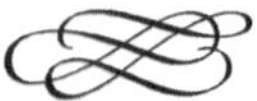

CHAPTER 3

The following Saturday, the first one in September, Moss arrived at Molly's surprisingly early for their date. He was a guy who liked to sleep in on the weekends, but it had been his suggestion they go hiking early in the day.

"Is this where you live?" Moss asked, surveying the tiny space with incredulity as he stepped into her apartment.

"No, this is the staging area I use so people don't feel uncomfortable with my vast wealth," Molly replied.

"It's nice," he said in a lame attempt to recover.

"Believe it or not, it's a lot nicer than anyplace else I've ever lived, and it's helping me save for the house I'm hoping to buy within the next five years."

"You have a five year plan? I don't even know what I'm going to be doing ten minutes from now," he said.

"You're going to be in the car with me," she replied, smiling. She had put more effort than usual into her appearance today, and Moss seemed to take note for the first time, doing an almost comical double take as he finally took stock of her. He stepped further into the apartment and came to rest dangerously close to her.

"Hey," he said.

"Hey," she replied. She clasped her hands behind her back and bounced lightly on her toes to relieve some of her nervous tension. It was finally happening, she was doing it; she was going on a date with Moss. *Don't blow it, don't blow it, don't blow it,* she warned herself. Moss liked the thrill of the hunt; it wouldn't do to toss herself at him and scare him away by being forward. "I packed stuff."

"Yeah? What sort of stuff?" he asked, still staring at her mouth.

"Some necessities for the hike," she told him and turned toward the kitchen to grab her backpack.

"You think of everything, Mol. I didn't even grab a water bottle."

"What are secretaries for?" she asked him.

"Probably not this," he said. His siblings would kill him if they knew what he was doing. And that was why he hadn't told a single member of his family what he was up to.

"Where exactly are we going today?" she asked.

"The Daniel Boone forest," he said. "Some friends told me about some cool hikes in there."

"I've never been. I should grab a jacket, in case it's cool in the shade," she said. She grabbed a jacket from the entry closet and, just in case, added a hoodie.

"You're so prepared. It's like watching a girl scout in action," he said.

"Were you ever in the scouts?" she asked.

"I tried it, but it didn't stick. Too many knots," he said.

She laughed. "That sounds about right."

"You know me so well," he said.

"And yet I like you anyway. What's *wrong* with me?" she said.

"Hey, you're supposed to be nice to me today. I'm letting you ride in my super cool car," he said.

"The Love Machine?"

"I forgot you knew I called it that," he said.

"I know all your secrets, Moss," she said.

"Well, not *all* my secrets," he said.

"I know your family, your salary, your work habits, all the girls you've dated the last three years, I've seen your medical records—what more is there?" she asked.

"Oh, Molly, Molly, Molly, you've only scratched the surface. I'm an ocean. Moss is the gift that keeps on giving."

"Wow," Molly said.

"See? You're blown away already," he said.

"We should go before I change my mind," Molly said.

He held the door for her, and the car door. His car was an orange Mustang from the seventies he had spent untold amounts of money and time restoring. Like his siblings, he was handy with anything that needed fixing, cars included. He had changed Molly's brakes for her the last time she needed them, saving her a few hundred in parts and labor. It was sweet things like that that had kept her hanging on over the years.

"Moss, can I ask you a question?" she said after they had been driving for a while. It had taken her that long to work up the nerve.

"What's that?" he said. He was only half listening. The rest of his attention was on the obscure indie band sounds now streaming from his phone.

"Why did you ask me out today? I mean, it's not like my interest in you has been a secret, and it's been three years."

"Because I finally feel ready for a change. I'm twenty five, and the girls I've been dating since high school haven't changed since high school, you know what I mean? There's a lot of crazy in the world, and you're not crazy. Crazy cute, maybe." He reached over the seat and squeezed her thigh, causing her to jump and squeal before shoving his hand away. "And crazy ticklish. What else don't I know about you, Mol, what are your secrets?"

"It would probably be easier to start with what you do know about me," she said. "Tell me, what do you know about Molly O'Ryan?" Maybe she was testing him, but she couldn't seem to help herself.

"I know you're cute," he said.

"You already mentioned."

"You're so cute I'm allowed to mention it twice. I know you fill out a bathing suit like," he kissed his fingertips and released them into the air, the Italian gesture for praise.

She sat waiting for him to say more.

"I know you're a good worker and my family loves you and you're sweet and thoughtful and loyal." He nodded approval at himself for being able to think of so much, but Molly wasn't feeling it. He had no idea where she was from or what her hobbies were, what her hopes and dreams were. On the other hand, he had just asked to know more about her, and this was their first date. Perhaps she was being too hard on him. Just because he hadn't been paying as much attention to her the last three years as she had paid to him didn't mean he wasn't ready to start now. She opened her mouth to tell him something about herself, but he grabbed his phone.

"Hey, I love this song. It's so great, listen."

She smiled and nodded, but she would never be as into music as he was. While he jammed along with his tune, she turned to look out the window at the passing scenery. They were already in the forest and going deeper, much deeper than she had ever been. Molly resisted the urge to shudder. It felt darker and colder and, though she would never admit as much to Moss, she had a secret fear of being lost in the woods. Or lost anywhere, for that matter.

"Where did you say this trail is?" she asked.

"It's up here somewhere. My buddy said we'd know it when we saw it," he replied.

"Do you have a map?" she asked.

He laughed. "A map for a trail? Do they even make that kind of thing?"

"Yes, it's called a, wait for it, trail map," she said. "I'm definitely beginning to see why the scouts took a pass on you."

"We'll figure it out," he said with the same amount of ease and confidence he used on everything in his life.

Approximately ten minutes later, he pulled off the road and turned off the car. "This is it."

Molly looked around. They were in the middle of nowhere with no discernable signs of life. "How do you know?"

"See that fallen tree with the weird branches? That's it."

"Okay," Molly said. It did almost look like there was a small trail leading into the woods, but it also might have been a deer path. "What happens if we see a bear?"

"We pray I can outrun you," he said, and she wasn't entirely sure he was joking. He took her hand and gave it a squeeze. "Come on, Mol, live a little."

"It's not the living part that bothers me, Moss; it's the possibility of dying," she said.

"Would I let anything happen to you?" he asked.

That was the problem; she had no idea. But she got out of the car, slipped her pack onto her back, and followed him to the trailhead. "This is going to be epic," he said. "I haven't had a day off in forever."

"Me, neither," she agreed. "My boss is such a jerk."

He turned around to smile at her with his trademark grin and took her hand, lacing their fingers together. "Yeah, that Joe, he's kind of evil," he agreed.

Molly laughed because Joe Samperi was one of the sweetest, kindest, gentlest men she had ever met.

"Ready?" Moss asked.

"Ready," Molly said, her heart fluttering wildly. It felt as if they were embarking on more than a hike, as if their journey into the woods was symbolic of the beginning of something more.

"Then let's go," Moss said, and they were off.

⚷

*B*efore stepping into the forest, the day had been bright and clear. After taking a few steps beneath the canopy, it felt dark and ominous. Molly shivered and paused to put on her hoodie.

"This is so cool," Moss said, his voice full of childlike enthusiasm. "Isn't it awesome to think we might be stepping where Daniel Boone actually once walked?"

"I didn't know you were that into Daniel Boone," she said.

"See? I told you you didn't know everything. I read tons of books on him when I was a kid, and I had a coonskin cap and a wooden gun. My mom thought those would be safer than cap guns, but we ended up beating each other over the head with them, so it probably didn't work out like she hoped."

"I've seen pictures of you in your coonskin cap," she told him. "Kind of adorable."

"I still have it. I'll wear it for you sometime, if that's what you're into," he said and gave her hand a squeeze.

She laughed. "It's so dark back here. I guess that's why it's called the 'dark and bloody ground.'"

"What? I've never heard that before. What's that supposed to mean?"

"Well, it's dark because of the forest. And the blood is presumably from all the battles that were fought here. Lots of Indian skirmishes, both before and after the settlers came," she said.

"Are you some kind of history buff?" he asked.

"No, but my family has lived near here for generations. My grandma told me lots of stories as a kid," she said. At the mention of her grandmother, her voice turned sad, but he didn't seem to notice and she was glad. There was no need to get into her tumultuous family history today. Or ever, if she could help it.

"That's so cool. I love it here, all these woods and creeks and trees. I can't even imagine what it would have been like if we had stayed in Brooklyn. Every time we go to visit my Nonna, I feel so claustrophobic," he said.

"I'm genuinely shocked, Moss. I had you pegged as a big city guy. I mean, you love music and shopping and bagels," she said.

"That's true, and I enjoy that aspect of our visits. But I definitely couldn't live there. Everything is so crowded together, and there's so much noise and traffic. I like being able to spread out and listen to birds and stuff. My favorite parts of childhood were running loose on our land, playing in the creek, turning over rocks. It was like the idyllic way to grow up, for a kid."

"Yeah," Molly agreed with more than a trace of envy. She loved the Samperis, loved everything about them. She loved their strong family bonds, their driving work ethic, the way they supported each other and had built a thriving business from nothing. They represented everything she had ever wanted in life. And, if she were being honest, she wasn't always sure whether her attraction to Moss served as a means to being part of them. Would she be as attracted to him if his last name was Smith? She tried never to peer too closely into that particular thought.

They hiked for a couple of hours and then stopped to eat the lunch Molly had packed. "I'm so glad you thought of food. I'm starving," Moss said.

Molly tried not to be self-conscious about her cooking, or lack thereof. No doubt Moss's mother, Mrs. Samperi, would have arrived with a ten-course spread and enough of it to feed a logging camp. Molly had packed sandwiches, fruit, chips, and store-bought cookies.

Moss finished his second sandwich, drained a bottle of water, and stretched. "I guess we should head back."

"Probably," Molly said, relieved and trying not to show it. It wasn't that she hadn't enjoyed the hike, because she had. But the darkness was getting to her, and more than once, she had wondered if she heard a bear. Moss, of course, had no such worries and stood reluctantly to his feet, leaving Molly to pick up his trash and stuff it back into her pack.

"Has it been epic?" she asked Moss as she stood and picked up her pack.

"Almost." His fingers brushed her face and he kissed her. It took a second for her to respond, so shocked was she. And then she dropped her pack, slid her arms around his neck, urged him closer, and kissed him in return. They stood in the small clearing of trees, kissing like teenagers for a very long time. For Molly, it felt as if all her pent up longing and desire for him was finally finding a release. And she liked the fact that everything remained PG. She could kiss him without the pressure of what might happen next. It was definitely the most fun she'd had with a guy since junior high school, when kissing was all she knew existed in the world.

At last Moss took a step back. "We should probably definitely be going now, or the sun is going to set." He sounded shaky and breathless and she couldn't resist standing on her toes to give him one last chaste peck on the lips.

"M'kay," she said.

"That's it? I just showed herculean restraint by stepping away from you, and all you have to say is m'kay?" he said.

"M'kay, you're a good kisser," she amended.

"That's better," he said. He picked up her pack, slid it onto his back, took her hand, and they set off.

CHAPTER 4

They had taken approximately five steps when both of them realized they had no idea which way to go.

"Um," Molly said, turning in a slow circle to try and retrace their steps. She would not panic, she would not panic.

"It was probably this way," Moss said, tugging her toward the left.

"This seems like the kind of thing we should probably be sure about," she said.

"I'm sure all paths lead somewhere eventually," he said.

She cocked her head to study him and see if he was serious. "There are like eleven hundred square miles here. We could be lost for days, maybe forever."

"Which one do you think it is?" he asked.

She turned back around, feeling the tightness of pressure in her chest. What if she got it wrong? "The sun was to our right when we came in. It was directly overhead when we started to eat. So we need to keep it to our right again."

"Lead on, Sacagawea," he said.

"Do you think that's right?" Molly asked.

"Sure," he said.

With more than a flicker of worry, Molly headed in the direction she thought they should go. They walked for about an hour and the flicker turned into a simmer and then a full boil.

"None of this looks familiar," she said, pausing to turn in a slow circle again. "There are so many deer paths."

"Or bear paths," Moss said.

"I'm trying very hard not to think about bears right now," Molly said.

"Then you should definitely not look over your left shoulder," Moss said. Molly spun and saw an adult bear approximately a hundred yards away, snuffling in the brush and ignoring them completely.

"We should keep moving," Moss whispered.

"But what if it's not the right way?" Molly asked.

"Any way that's opposite of him is the right way," Moss said. He took her hand and they began walking again.

Ninety minutes later, the sun began to sink lower on the horizon, and Molly had to fight hard not to panic.

"I'm hungry," Moss announced.

Uh-oh, Molly thought. Moss and hunger did not go well together. Deprived of food, he behaved the way some addicts did when deprived of drugs. He became cranky, whiny, and unreasonable. He was the reason she always kept a supply of almonds and granola bars in her desk drawer. The last time he was hungry at work, nearly two years ago, he had exploded at her over a misunderstanding. Molly had gone into the bathroom and cried. They hadn't spoken for two days, until Joe found out what happened and made Moss apologize.

"I have some granola bars in my bag," Molly said. She had no idea how long that would be able to stave off his grouchiness, but hopefully it would buy them enough time to get back to the car.

"I ate those an hour ago," he told her.

"All four of them?" she asked, trying hard to tamp down her frustration.

"I was hungry," he said, as if she weren't.

"I'm sorry, but that was all the food I packed."

"You should have packed more," he said.

"I packed a whole lot more than you did, which was nothing," she said.

"How did I know we were going to get lost?" Moss said.

"How could we not have gotten lost with such genius directions as 'start by the big tree.' They're all big trees!"

"Hey, you could have planned something. You know I'm bad at planning things," he said.

"You told me you had it covered. I was trying not to be controlling," she snapped.

"I like it when you're controlling," he snapped back. "I hate being in charge of stuff, Molly, you know that."

"I cannot believe you are blaming this on me," she said.

They stamped through the woods a while longer in silence, until it grew so dark that they began to trip on branches. At last Molly stopped again. "I think we're going to have to stop here for the night."

"You mean like sleep here, in the woods?" Moss said.

"Yes, that's what I mean."

"But we have no food," Moss said.

"We'll have to go hungry. I'm sure we can find our way out at daybreak, but if we keep going now we're either going to get more lost or hurt ourselves on something."

"I knew it was the other way. I should never have listened to you," he said grumpily.

"Well, you did, so suck it up and look for a spot to settle down for the night," she said. She yanked her backpack away from him, sat down, and began rifling through it.

"What are you doing? Do you have more food?"

"There's no more food, Moss," she said. "I'm looking for my emergency supply pack."

"What's in it?" he sank onto the piney floor across from her, his face hopeful.

"Matches, a couple of foil blankets, a flashlight, and some emergency medical supplies."

"Great, let's build a fire," he said.

She looked around the impenetrable forest. "There's no clearing," she said.

"So?"

"So I don't want to burn down the forest. Plus it's too dense and wet to even get started. Fires take preparation. Let's just find a sheltered spot and huddle up."

"But it's so cold," Moss complained, running his hands up and down his bare arms.

With a sigh, Mollie removed her hoodie and handed it to him. Meanwhile she put on her jacket, which was much lighter weight than her hoodie had been. Moss slipped her hoodie over his head, plucked it to his nose, and sniffed it. "Smells like you," he said with a slight smile.

"Super," Molly said. At this moment, romance was the very last thing on her mind. "I have to go."

"You're leaving me?" he asked, sounding like a little boy whose mom was heading off to work for the first time.

"No, I mean I have to *go*." She held up the roll of toilet paper she'd packed. "You stay here and don't move. I'll be right back." She took the flashlight and headed approximately twenty feet away.

"Molly," Moss called almost as soon as she had walked away.

"Yes," she answered.

"Just checking. I don't like to be alone."

"No one does when it's this dark," she replied.

"I wonder what my mom is making for supper," he said. He pulled out his phone and held it up, hoping for a signal. They had been trying to get a signal the last few hours with no luck. "How can there not be any cell towers here? What century is this. Molly?" he added when she didn't answer.

The flashlight was in her teeth and she couldn't. She needed a couple more hands to balance herself, maintain control of the flashlight, and hold the toilet paper. Men were so lucky; they would never know the trauma of having to squat in a darkened forest, wondering what creatures might be scurrying beneath you.

"Molly," Moss said again, and it sounded as if he were moving.

"Stay still," Molly called and the flashlight dropped to the forest floor and clicked off. She finished her business and spent an inordinate amount of time trying to find the light, all the while talking to Moss in soothing tones so he wouldn't dart away and become more lost.

She found the flashlight, returned to Moss, and rooted through her pack for the hand sanitizer she'd packed. "Let's scout a good spot to settle," she said when it became clear Moss had no intention of taking the lead and was waiting on her to do so.

He nodded and stood. She clasped his hand and began leading him in a small circle, the flashlight sweeping around in an arc. Eventually she located a downed pine tree that had broken in half. Beneath the tree was piney and soft and the two halves of the trunk had created a sort of rough, two-sided dwelling. "There," she said. She led Moss over to it and set down her pack, clearing away some pinecones. "Do you want to lay one of the foil blankets on the ground to sleep on or do you want to sleep on the ground and put both blankets over us?" she asked.

"I dunno, whatever," he said, shrugging.

Molly repressed another sigh. *This must be what it feels like to be lost in the woods with a child,* she thought. "The ground is moist and that will make us colder. Let's put down one of the blankets as a vapor barrier and share the other one."

He stood by while she opened the first foil blanket and spread it on the ground. "Lie down," she instructed, and he did. She lay down beside him, unwrapped the other blanket, and spread it on top of them.

"I'm so hungry," he reiterated. Molly didn't chime in to tell him how hungry and thirsty she was because what was the point? They wouldn't be eating until at least the next day.

"We should sleep. It will conserve energy," she said.

He was quiet for a minute before he spoke again. "Want to, you know, do stuff?"

"Really, really not," she said. She had never been less attracted to him, and she felt gross, sweaty and smelly, with teeth that felt like they were covered in fur coats.

"Fine," he said, pouting. He tugged the foil blanket and wrapped it around himself, thereby ripping it away from her. She kicked him.

"Ouch," he exclaimed.

"I'm cold too, you know. Stop hogging the blanket." She yanked the blanket back.

"I'm bigger," he argued.

"It's my blanket," she said.

"Wow, that is so selfish," he said.

Molly pressed back a thousand harsh replies. It wouldn't help anything to take out her frustration on him. "Go to sleep," she said in a softer tone. "Things will be better in the morning."

"Can we at least spoon?" he asked.

"Do I get to be the little spoon?" she replied.

"Just this once," he said. He snugged up against her and draped his arm over her waist.

She scooted back slightly, adjusting their fit. "Goodnight," she whispered.

He pushed aside her hair and pressed a kiss to the back of her neck. "Good night."

CHAPTER 5

In the morning, Molly woke shivering at first light. Her blanket was gone. She sat up and spied Moss, completely cocooned in their lone blanket. Quietly, she rifled in the pack for the toilet paper and went into the woods. When she returned, Moss was still sleeping. She considered letting him sleep, but she also knew that, on his days off, he tended to sleep until well after noon. She nudged him with her foot. He blinked sleepily up at her and then frowned resentfully.

"What?" he said.

"We should probably get going. The sooner we find the car, the sooner we can get back to civilization and food."

He sat up and ran his hand through his messy mop of curls. Molly could only imagine what she looked like. She sorted through her pack until she found her bag of toiletries and then combed her hair and secured it with a tie before dabbing on a little lip balm. She used her fingers to wipe away any gunk from under her eyes and spritzed on a tiny amount of grapefruit-scented body spray. It probably wouldn't be able to do much against the lack of deodorant, but at least she didn't feel so grimy and gross, for the moment.

Moss was watching her. "It's not fair you make yourself look all cute and then I'm not allowed to touch you," he pouted.

"I think cute must be a relative opinion. I feel gross."

"Well, you look adorable," he groused, as if her attempts at hygiene were somehow a personal attack on him. He looked pretty cute himself, for someone having just woken up with a mop of tousled curls sliding over his brows. He pushed them back again and stood up. "I've never gone this long without eating before. I feel yack."

Molly stayed quiet. She had gone this long without eating before, and then some, but now wasn't the time to try and one up him. "Maybe you'll feel better once we start moving," she said.

"I won't," he insisted. "I have to use the bathroom." He turned his back on her and unzipped his pants.

"Geez, Moss," Molly said, turning her back, too. "You couldn't take ten steps away from our campsite?"

"I'm too hungry and weak," he said. She heard him zip his pants and turned back around.

"Here," she said, handing him the bottle of hand sanitizer before he could ask. She really didn't want to find out if he never intended to ask for it.

Molly had spent some time the night before thinking about the position of the sun, relative to the position of the sun when they first arrived. She hoped today it would be easier to duplicate their position based on the time of day they arrived versus the time of late afternoon they had left. She cinched up her pack and slid it on her back, preparing to start, when Moss spoke.

"I want to lead today," he declared.

"I think I might know where we are now," she said.

"That was what you said yesterday," he said.

"No, it wasn't. I asked for your input yesterday, and you didn't have any," she said.

"Now I do," he said.

"Fine, which way do you think we should go?" she asked.

He pointed in the opposite direction of the way she had been thinking.

"I don't think that's right," she said.

"I say it is," he said.

"I say you're wrong," she said.

"You don't know," he said.

"I know better than you. We want to go this way, it's the way we came," she said.

"Fine, let's split up. You go the way you think and I'll go the way I think and we'll see which one is right," he said. He took a step away from her. She grabbed the back of his pants and held him back.

"Let me get this straight," she said. "You're so convinced of your rightness that you're willing to let me go off and die to prove your point."

"That's the same thing you're doing," he said.

"No, it's not. I want us to stay together so, no matter what, we have each other. I would never send you off alone into the forest because I'm mad at you or because I think I'm right and you're wrong."

"I guess that's the difference between us," he said, crossing his arms over his chest.

Molly pressed her fingers to her temple. She was about to go nuclear on him. She hated to do it, but it was a life-or-death situation. "Mossimo Samperi, you are going to go my way or, so help me, when we get out of here, I will tell your mother every lousy thing you have ever said or done, and I mean ever."

"You wouldn't," he said.

She quirked an eyebrow. "Try me."

They stared each other down until at last he caved. "Fine, I'll go your way, but if we die, it's all your fault." Shoulders slumping, he trailed after her as she pounded through the forest, furious and in a hurry to get the horrible ordeal of the date over with.

After about an hour, they emerged onto the road. "The car's not here, genius," he said.

She shaded her eyes and looked up, trying to push through the disorienting bog of low blood sugar. "This way," she said, pointing to the left. After about a quarter of a mile, they stumbled upon the car. Moss ran over to it and laid his body against it.

"My baby, Daddy is so happy to see you." He pressed a couple of kisses to the car and smiled at Molly. She was probably supposed to be amused at his display, but she was annoyed. There was no recognition of the fact that she had been right or that she had safely led them out of the forest and back to the car.

"Can we go now?" she asked.

"Fine, fine," he said, all smiles now that the danger had passed. He pulled out his keys and unlocked the door. Molly slid inside and buckled her safety belt.

"I saw a *McDonalds* about ten miles back," she said.

"Sounds good," he agreed. He turned the key. Nothing happened. Molly closed her eyes and pressed her lips together, hoping it was some sort of bad dream. He tried the engine again. Nothing happened.

"Oh," he said, sitting back.

"What's the problem?" she asked through gritted teeth.

"I think my battery is dead. I've needed a new one and haven't gotten around to it. Oops."

Miraculously, Molly refrained from comment. She pulled out her phone and held it aloft. She had no bars.

"Try your phone," she said. They had different service plans and his phone had had service when they arrived. He pulled out his phone, but it was dead.

"I guess I shouldn't have listened to so much music yesterday. Oops," he said.

Molly rubbed at the spot between her eyes. They were miles and miles from anywhere. It was a long, deserted road, highly unlikely to receive any traffic. His phone was dead, and hers had no signal. What to do?

Moss reached across her and opened the glove compartment. Sifting inside, he came away with a mint. "Want to split it?" he asked.

She blinked at his calm, measured tone. "Don't you think we should figure out what we're going to do?" she asked.

"It'll be fine," he said. "Someone will find us."

"This is not a highly traveled road," she informed him.

He tapped the dash of his car. "GPS."

"What?"

"My car has GPS installed. Someone will be along soon," he said.

Molly didn't understand until, less than five minutes later, a car arrived, a car she recognized. Moss's older brother, Benny, and his fiancée, Lou, pulled up and rolled down the window.

"Dead battery?" Benny guessed.

"Yep," Moss said.

Lou crawled across Benny and stuck her head out the window. "Molly, is that you?"

"Hi," Molly said with a sheepish wave. It embarrassed her in ways she couldn't articulate that Lou should see her sitting there. Lou was so together, so powerful and professional. She was the sort of woman Molly always thought she could be, with the right opportunities and encouragement. To have Lou see her in a compromising position with Moss, her one weakness, was humiliating.

"Hop in," Benny said. "We'll take Molly home and send a tow for your car."

Molly got out of Moss's car and slid into the back seat of Benny's. It was a new car, one he recently purchased after deciding he would stay in the states.

"What were you guys doing?" Lou asked.

Moss launched into a long story of their date, playing up the adventurous parts and leaving out the parts where they probably would have stabbed each other if they'd had access to weapons. Molly remained quiet. Every once in a while, Lou darted her anxious glances, and so did Benny. Thankfully, neither of them said anything.

They drove through *McDonalds* and loaded up on coffee and food.

"How did you find us?" Molly asked after she had eaten and the hunger-induced fog began to clear from her brain.

"The GPS in Moss's car," Benny explained. "Mom checked it this morning when he didn't come home. You're lucky she didn't send the cavalry. It was only Dad who intervened and sent me instead."

Molly's glance slid to Moss. "Your mom monitors the GPS on your car?"

"In case I get stuck or in trouble or something, which worked out well for us this morning," he said, nudging her with his elbow.

She turned to stare out the window. *Wow,* she thought, *wow.* When she faced forward again, Lou caught her eye in the mirror and raised her eyebrows as if to say, *"Do you understand what you're in for?"*

"I know, right?" Molly tried to say back with a look of her own, but she wasn't sure Lou got it. Maybe later she would have a chance to talk to her about the weirdness of a twenty-five-year-old man's mother keeping tabs on him. It was all a little too Norman Bates for her taste.

The ride back to her house was long. Molly resisted the urge to fall asleep, but it took every ounce of self-control to stay awake. Moss didn't even try to do it. He fell asleep almost as soon as he finished his food and began to snore softly. He was still asleep when they reached Molly's apartment, and she was relieved.

"Let him sleep," she told Benny when he would have woken Moss to say goodbye to her. "Thank you guys so much for coming to get us, I really appreciate it."

Benny turned to look at her. "Are you all right, Molly?"

"I'm fine," Molly said and realized she meant it. She smiled to show him it was true. For the first time in a long time, she felt free, as if the disaster date with Moss had somehow broken a long-held fever and she could move on and recover now. "See you at work tomorrow. Bye, Lou."

"I'll call you, we'll have lunch," Lou said. Molly could tell she was dying to know the inside story of what went down and how Molly was feeling about everything.

"Sounds good," Molly said. She gave them a little wave, sprinted up the sidewalk to her apartment, let herself in, and crashed into a dead sleep for the next four hours.

On Monday, Molly woke feeling groggy yet cheerful. She would have the office to herself, sparing any awkward encounters with Moss. Even Benny was out of the office, having taken a day off to do wedding errands with Lou. The day was productive, with no interruptions from the Samperis. In a few weeks, production would begin on their television show, so now felt like crunch time trying to finish projects and get everything in order. Molly barely knew how to hold a hammer, but she loved that her efficiency in the office enabled them to go out and do what they did best. It made her feel like she was an actual part of the team, even if she wasn't the one tearing down walls and pouring concrete.

She was about to sign out for the day when Moss arrived and handed her a small plant. "For your desk," he explained.

"Thank you, that's so sweet," she said. They shared a smile. Molly took a breath and jumped in before she lost her nerve. "About this weekend, I wanted you to know I meant what I said. We'll go back to being friends with no hard feelings or awkwardness."

He frowned. "What are you talking about?"

"We said if things didn't work out, we wouldn't let it come between us. I'm telling you we're good, no harm, no foul."

"I came here to see if you wanted to go out tonight," he said.

"Why?" she blurted.

"Because that's what people do when they're dating," he said.

"Moss, did we have the same date this weekend? It was horrible," she said.

"What are you talking about? It was awesome," he said. "It was probably the best, most exciting date I've ever had."

"Which part? The part where we got lost in the woods for hours with no food, the part where we argued like an old married couple, or the part where—when we finally found the car—we had to wait for your big brother to come get us?" she asked.

"What about the part where we stood in the forest and kissed for the better part of an hour?" he said, his fingers brushing her cheek.

She took a step back away from his touch. "That part was pretty great. I just don't think we're in the same place."

"We're both right here," he said.

"I was speaking metaphorically. I think we want different things right now," she said.

"I want to be with you, don't you want to be with me?" he asked.

She twisted her fingers together, feeling more than a little distress. She had thought she and Moss were on the same page after their terrible first date. It had never occurred to her that he might want a repeat. "You are into your music and your car and hanging out. I want a little more than that."

"What do you want? I will totally give it to you," he said.

"I've spent most of my life taking care of myself. I don't want to have to take care of someone else," she said, as gently as she could.

"What are you talking about? No one has to take care of me," he said.

Your mom does. She refrained from blurting the obvious truth, knowing he wasn't ready to hear it. "I'm not trying to hurt your feelings, but I'm trying to be honest with you so there's no misunderstanding between us. You're still my friend, and you're still my boss. I'll go on working happily here until eternity. But I want someone a little more responsible and a little more mature."

"What?" he exclaimed, aghast. "I am totally mature and responsible."

The front door opened then and a middle-aged woman entered. In one hand she carried a large bag and, in the other, a car seat with a baby inside.

"May I help you?" Molly asked but she ignored Molly and focused on Moss.

"Are you Moss?" she asked.

"Yes," he said, frowning in confusion.

She shoved the baby at him. "Here, this is yours."

Moss took the giant car seat but he didn't look at the baby. His mouth was slack with shock. "What? What are you talking about?"

"Remember Tammy? You went out about nine months ago."

Moss seemed to be searching his memory bank, and Molly wanted to punch him. How could he not remember someone he had obviously been intimate with? "Yes, okay, Tammy, right. She called herself Love Moon."

The woman rolled her eyes. "She does that sometimes. She was clean while she was pregnant, but she fell off the wagon a couple of weeks ago, after the baby was born. We were going to keep the baby, but I can't deal with her and a daughter on heroin." Her voice broke. She took a breath and tried to compose herself. "She's a good baby. I wrote down her schedule and packed up all her stuff, along with a can of formula. Here, her name is Bella." She slid the bag toward him and turned away, tears streaking her face. She didn't allow herself to glance at the baby or say goodbye before she let herself out of the office. When she was gone, Molly and Moss stared at each other in silence.

Moss set the baby carrier down, still without looking inside. It was as if he didn't look at it, then it wasn't true. "What just happened?" he muttered.

"I think you just became a dad," Molly said. Unlike Moss, she was incredibly curious about the baby. She got down on her knees and peered at the little bundle who, under her cap, had a tousled mop of brown curls. "Oh, yeah, she's yours."

"That's not funny," Moss said.

"I'm not joking," Molly said. "She looks just like you. Look at her little nose." She slid a finger down the baby's tiny, straight nose. She was beautiful, completely and totally perfect, and she was Moss's, with some other woman. Despite her decision not to have anything more to do with him, the knowledge of this baby's existence stuck like a dagger in her heart. Still, it wasn't the baby's fault. Molly unfastened the buckles of the car seat, pulled the baby out, and cuddled her close, sniffing the intoxicating newborn aroma drifting from her head. She looked clean and well fed, both good signs.

"What do you know about this Tammy girl?" Molly asked. The baby scent was delicious, and Molly closed her eyes, inhaling deeply. Her hormones were fully awake now and doing battle inside her. She needed a baby of her own, pronto. She took a breath and shook her head, pushing back the storm of estrogen brewing in her body.

"We went out a few times. She used to hang out at *Truckers*. One night after a concert…it was a one-time thing. I felt really bad about it. I don't usually do stuff like that, Molly, I swear. I'm not a one-night-stand type of guy."

Apparently you were at least one night, she thought, but refrained from saying it. He sat down and put his head in his hands, in shock.

"What am I going to tell my family?" he asked, rocking back and forth. He meant what was he going to tell his mother, Molly knew. The rest of the family wouldn't care, except maybe Joe and Peaches, for whom the infant would represent an enormous amount of pain.

"Suck it up, Moss. You can do this. This baby needs you," Molly said.

He looked up at her, horrified. "What are you talking about? I can't keep it. I can barely keep myself together, you just said it. I'm only twenty five."

"And she's only two weeks. Look at her."

He shook his head and closed his eyes. "Maybe you could keep her," he said.

Molly was tempted. She knew what it was to be alone and adrift in the world. She had always thought one day she might try to do foster care or adopt. But this baby wasn't alone in the world. She had Moss and, by extension, all of the Samperis. "This is your child, Moss, your responsibility." Despite her words, she sat and cuddled the baby close to her chin, rocking her gently.

"I don't know what to do," he said, his head still in his hands. "Tell me what to do."

"Take her home, introduce her to your parents," she said, her tone gentle because she had never seen him freak out this badly before.

"How am I supposed to get her home?" Moss asked. "She can't fit in the back of my car."

That part was true. Moss's car had only two doors. The back seat was shallow and lacking seatbelts. It would never hold a car seat. "I'll drive her home for you," Molly volunteered.

"Will you come inside with me? I need the moral support," he said.

"I'll come with you," she promised, but there was a lot of selfishness in her words. She had started the story, and now she wanted to see how it ended; she wanted to see how the Samperis reacted to the news. "But first, hold out your hands."

He held out his hands as if waiting for candy, not realizing what she intended to do until she placed the baby into them. "Congratulations, Dad, it's a girl."

Instinctively, he brought the baby close to his chest and cradled her, staring down at her little face for the first time. "I always thought I would be pretty as a girl. Guess I was right," he said. He swiped his eyes on his elbow, and Molly went all mushy inside. Finally, *finally,* maybe this would be the impetus he needed to grow up. She leaned down and pressed a tender kiss to his lips and he clung to her a few seconds until the baby started to squirm.

"I'm going to figure out how to buckle this into my car," she said, picking up the car seat.

"You're not going to leave me alone with her," he said, panicked.

"Only for a minute," she said and jogged to her car where she spent a ridiculous amount of time trying to figure out how to affix the complicated mechanism into her vehicle. Finally she realized the seat detached from a base unit that clicked and latched in her back seat.

After that she put the seat back together, tightened it, and went to retrieve the baby.

When she went inside, the baby was howling and Moss stood in the middle of the room, a deer in headlights expression on his face. "She's screaming. Make her stop." He practically shoved the baby back at Molly who rifled through the bag one-handed until she found the baby's schedule.

"She's hungry, I have to make her a bottle," she said. She shoved the baby back at Moss and quickly prepared a bottle using formula and a pre-measured container of water she found in one of the side pockets. When the formula was ready, she took the baby back from Moss and started to feed the baby who sucked greedily at the tiny nipple. Molly wasn't an expert on babies, but she knew a baby was supposed to be burped at some point. After she'd had about a quarter of the bottle, she set it aside, tipped the baby over her shoulder, and patted her back until she emitted a delicate belch. After the burp, the baby squirmed as if she were still hungry, so Molly fed her the rest of the bottle and burped her again. Moss sat in her chair and watched as if it were a documentary on an exotic species he had never encountered before.

"I can't do this," he said as Molly checked the baby's diaper, found it dry, and wrapped her back up in her blankets. "Look at you, you already know what to do with her. I have no idea. I'm going to break her."

"You're not going to break her; you're going to learn what to do with her. You'll figure it out," she said. "Come on, let's go."

Reluctantly, he followed her outside and stood by while she buckled the baby into the back of her car. She followed him to his house and unfastened the baby when they parked in front of the large house. He made no offer to take the baby's carrier from her, and Molly didn't insist. He'd had a shock, and she was already dreading saying goodbye to the tiny bundle. They walked in the front door. The house, as usual, smelled like tomatoes and garlic, a smell Molly found immensely comforting.

Moss led the way to the kitchen, where Mrs. Samperi could almost always be found. As expected, she stood with her back to them, stirring a large, bubbling pot.

"You're home early, son," she commented without turning around. She always seemed to have a sixth sense about which of her children was in the room, though Molly guessed it wasn't a difficult deduction to make these days since only Moss lived at home, along with Benny who was staying put until his upcoming wedding.

"Molly's here," Moss announced.

Mrs. Samperi turned to her with a smile. "Wonderful, I hope you can stay for supper, dear." Her eyes fell on the baby, and her smile widened. "Is this your niece?"

Molly wasn't sure how to answer. She looked to Moss who seemed similarly dumbfounded. She poked him. He cleared his throat. "Dad, can you come in here?" he called. His father appeared a minute later, smiling when he saw Molly.

"Molly girl, nice to see you. I hope you'll stay for supper," Mr. Samperi said.

"Pete, something's wrong," his wife said, her eyes scanning between Molly and Moss with eagle-like precision.

"Um, Mom, Dad, this is kind of hard to say, but a while ago there was this girl and, um," his eyes landed on the baby. "She's mine."

His parents stared at him, uncomprehending. Then they turned to Molly, as if she might offer some explanation. She remained quiet, trying hard to ooze support with her silence.

"What did you say?" Mrs. Samperi finally asked. "You got a girl in trouble?"

"Apparently," Moss said, dejected. "But I didn't know until today."

"Who is she? Where is she?" Mr. Samperi asked.

"Well, um, apparently she has a drug problem," Moss said.

"Are you on drugs?" Mr. Samperi asked.

"Dad, no, how could you ask me that?" Moss said.

"It's a lot to take in, Mossimo," Mr. Samperi said. He put his hand to his head. "What are we going to do?"

"I'll tell you what we're going to do," Mrs. Samperi said. She wiped her hands on a towel and set it aside. "We're going to raise her like one of our own, and she's going to be the most-loved little girl in the world. Let me see her."

Molly wasn't sure who the command was directed at, but she set the carrier down, knelt and unbuckled Bella. When she had pulled her out and straightened her clothes, she handed her to Mrs. Samperi who took her and cradled her close, her eyes sparkling with tears and her face smiling with delight.

"She looks just like you when you were a baby," she said, stroking her finger down the baby's cheek. Moss stepped closer and looked at the baby over his mother's shoulder, as if it was safe to get close to her now that he had his mother as a buffer. Beside them, Mr. Samperi and Molly locked eyes. Molly couldn't have put a name to the emotion that passed between them, but it felt something like concern. When he turned to look at the baby, she eased out of the room and drove home.

CHAPTER 7

The next day, all the Samperi siblings were in the office. They had to get their paperwork in, in preparation for payroll and billing. It was usually a festive, party atmosphere when everyone was in the office. Today an undercurrent of tension ran through the building, and no one seemed to be speaking. Joe didn't set foot outside his office, and no one tried to go behind his closed door, a door that usually remained opened.

"Where's the baby?" Molly asked Moss when he breezed through her office early in the day.

"My mom's taking care of her," Moss said. Behind him, Jessamine and Giovanni made eye contact and shared a frown. "Want to go out tonight?"

"I can't," Molly said, confused. She had a bookkeeping client scheduled after work, and she had figured Moss would want to spend the time getting to know his child, or at least giving his mother a break from all-day babysitting.

"Fine," Moss said grumpily, stalking off to his office. The entire building was a doublewide trailer that had been converted. Molly sat in the entryway, the greeting card of the company and the only person without walls and a door. Each sibling had his or her own office and then there was a large supply closet.

At noon, Lou stopped by. "Did I know you were coming?" Benny asked.

"How could you forget about me?" Lou said, then, "I'm joking. I came to take Molly to lunch."

Molly practically hopped out of her chair and sprinted to Lou's car. The atmosphere in the office was oppressive and nerve-wracking. It was the worst day she could remember since she started working for the family, and that was saying a lot because they were a family who believed in hashing out loud, vocal disagreements.

Lou waited to speak until they were safely tucked in her car. "Can you even believe it?" she exclaimed as soon as both doors were closed.

"No," Molly exploded. "You could cut the tension with a knife in there."

"Oh, I know. Benny called me last night after the big family melee."

"Did everyone come over and have it out?" Molly asked.

"Everyone but Joe and Peaches. Joe still hasn't said a word to anyone about anything," Lou said.

"That's not like him," Molly said. "He must be hurting pretty bad."

"Or Peaches is and he didn't want to say anything to make it worse," Lou said. Everyone knew, but no one discussed, the fact that Joe and Peaches seemed unable to have children. "What do you know about the girl?"

"I looked her up on Facebook last night. She's really, really pretty, and she seems like a good girl who got caught up in the opioid epidemic."

"Leave it to Moss to knock up a drug addict," Lou said. "I swear, that kid. Speaking of Moss, what's up between you two?"

"It's a mess," Molly said and filled Lou in on their disaster date, as well as her newfound desire not to have anything to do with him.

"So now you don't like Moss, but Moss likes you, and he needs you more than ever because he found out he's a daddy," Lou summarized.

"Pretty much," Molly agreed. "Although it doesn't seem to be affecting his life at all."

Lou rolled her eyes. "I told Benny to tell him to sew up permanent custody so the baby's mom won't be able to get her back and place her in danger. Benny's words were, 'Good luck getting her out of Ma's hands. She hadn't put her down all night.'"

"Mrs. Samperi to the rescue," Molly said.

"Exactly. I don't think Moss has ever had to face the consequence of a decision in his entire life," Lou said.

"How did the rest of them turn out so well?" Molly asked.

"There were so many of them, they had to learn to be independent. Then Moss came along and I think she realized he was the baby and she'd better hang on tight because he was the last one."

"And, boy, did she hang on tight," Molly said.

"He's probably the first kid in history where the mother tried to stuff him back into the womb," Lou said, and then put her hand over her mouth. "I should not be talking about my future mother-in-law this way."

"And I should not be talking about my boss's mother this way," Molly agreed.

"We should talk about her over food," Lou said.

"Definitely," Molly agreed, and they went to lunch.

When she returned to the office, Joe had left for the day, and Benny was attempting to moderate an argument between Giovanni, Jessamine, and Moss.

"Do you even understand what you're doing to Mom and Dad?" Jessamine yelled at Moss.

"What are you talking about? Mom has never been happier, she finally has a granddaughter," Moss yelled.

"She's not supposed to be raising her grandchild," Giovanni yelled. "She already raised five kids."

"She's happy," Moss yelled.

"Dad's not," Jessamine yelled. "They fought last night, did you know? Or were you too busy playing video games to notice?"

"It's not my fault they were fighting," Moss yelled.

"They were fighting over you," Jessamine yelled.

The yelling was nothing new, Samperis yelled practically everything they said to each other. But the subject matter was darker and more serious than anything Molly had heard them argue about before. She would have left, but they were standing in her portion of the office. Instead she slipped around behind them, sat down, and tried to be as unobtrusive as possible.

"What do you want me to do, quit my job to take care of a baby?" Moss said.

"Find an actual babysitter during the day and take care of her yourself at night," Giovanni said.

"Is that what you would do?" Moss asked.

"I don't have to think about it because I'm married, so if I have kids, Vivian and I will handle it together," Giovanni said.

"It's not my fault this happened," Moss yelled.

"It's absolutely your fault this happened," Jessamine yelled.

"You think nothing is ever your fault," Giovanni chimed in, yelling.

Moss turned to Benny. "Aren't you going to step in here?"

"So far, Moss, I kind of agree with them. You made a mess, and you need to clean it up yourself."

"Isn't anyone on my side?" Moss asked. He turned to Molly who tried to shrink into her chair.

"Molly doesn't count, this is between family," Jessamine yelled.

Molly bit her lip to keep it from trembling. Of course Jessamine was correct, she wasn't family. But she so desperately wanted to be that sometimes she fooled herself into believing she was one of them. She faced her computer and tried to drown them out and do work.

"Maybe we should take this into my office," Benny suggested. "I'm sorry, Molly, we didn't mean to disturb you."

She gave him a half smile, not trusting herself to speak. He seemed to know her feelings had been hurt. Of all of them, Benny and Joe were the most sensitive. If Joe were here, the fight wouldn't even be happening. He had a fatherly way of clamping down on disagreements, but Joe wasn't there. He was off nursing his own hurts, hurts that had been caused by Moss and his carelessness. She wanted to shake him for upsetting everyone so. But she couldn't; she had no right. She wasn't family.

Later that night, Molly finished her solitary salad and sat on the couch to read until she dozed. She woke herself up and went to bed and, for the first time in years, had nightmares. Later she couldn't remember what the dream was about, only that she was lost, scared and alone and running. Her feet pounded the pavement until she woke up, drenched and panting. She sat up, and the pounding continued. Someone was knocking on her front door. A glance at the clock showed it to be midnight.

She struggled out of the twisted covers, peered through her peephole, and opened the door. Moss and his baby stood on the other side.

"What are you doing here?" she said.

"Can I come in?" he asked. He sounded completely unlike himself —exhausted and more upset than she had ever heard him.

She moved aside as he made his way in. He set down the baby carrier and bag. "My parents kicked me out," he said.

Of all the things she had expected him to say, that hadn't even been on the list. "What? Why?"

"Apparently they've been fighting about the baby. My dad said she's not their responsibility and they're not going to raise her. They told me to leave and…and I'm not allowed to contact them for two months until I get my act together."

"What did your mom say?" she asked.

"Nothing. I think she and Dad had been fighting. Apparently he won."

"Wow, that's…I'm sorry?" she said, but it came out like a question. She wasn't sorry. Rather, she thought it was probably the best thing that had ever happened to him. Of course he wouldn't see it that way now or maybe ever. But at least now he had a chance.

"I know I have no right to ask, but can I stay here? I have nowhere else to go. Joe and Peaches—I can't. And Giovanni or Jessamine—I won't. And my friends—I can't take a baby there." He glanced down at the baby as if still surprised by her continued appearance in his life.

"Okay," she said, shocked and confused. "The guest room is empty of furniture, but you can crash on the couch. Did you bring a bed for the baby?"

"I brought the bassinet my mom bought. They let me take all her stuff, plus whatever stuff of mine I wanted, except my video game console."

"I'll help you carry things in and get her settled," she said. She followed him outside and saw he had brought one of his dad's pickup trucks. The back was loaded with random things—the bassinet, his guitar, an amp, and a couple of bags of what she presumed were his clothes. She helped him carry everything in. The baby began to stir.

"Is she hungry?" Molly asked.

"I have no idea," Moss said, sounding weary. He sat and made no move to pick up his child.

"When did she last eat?" Molly said.

"I don't know. My mom fed her," he said.

The baby's plaintive cries grated on her. She wanted to rush over, pick her up, and soothe her. But she knew if she did, a precedent would be established. Moss would transfer care of Bella from his mom to her, and he would never take responsibility for her.

"Get up and make her a bottle," Molly commanded.

"I'm tired," he whined.

"So am I, and so is she. But she's also hungry, and it's your responsibility to feed her."

"I don't know how to make a bottle," he said. "What if I do it wrong?"

"There are instructions on the formula can. Follow them exactly, and I'll oversee you to make sure it goes okay," she said.

With a sigh, he stood, rooted in the baby's bag, pulled out a bottle and formula and proceeded to combine them. Molly watched, ready to step in if he needed help, but, as she had suspected, he did fine on his own.

"Now what do I do?" he asked.

"Pick her up and feed her," Molly said.

"Can't you do it?" he asked.

"Yes, I can. And, no, I won't. You can do this; it's not so scary. Just make sure she's not getting too much because she can choke."

"Oh, that's not scary at all," he said sarcastically, but he unbuckled the baby from her car seat, sat on the couch with her, and started to feed her.

"You have to take the bottle out and burp her when it's about halfway finished," Molly said.

"How do I do that?" he asked.

"Hold her up on your shoulder, like this," she took the baby and positioned her on his shoulder. "Now pat her back to help her get the air out. Babies can't get trapped air out on their own, and it hurts them."

He dutifully patted the baby who, predictably, burped. Unpredictably, she spit up a large amount of formula on his shirt. "That's disgusting," he said, holding the baby away from him with a grimace.

"It happens a lot, I'm afraid. Here." She rifled through the bag until she found a burp cloth and cleaned both of them off.

He fed the baby the rest of the bottle, without being told, and then burped her again, putting the cloth beneath her to catch any spit up. "Now what?" he said when the burp had emerged.

"Now check her diaper to make sure she's dry and clean, and then you can put her to bed," Molly said.

"Hallelujah," Moss replied. He opened the baby's diaper and gagged. "It looks like mustard threw up. What's wrong with her?"

"Nothing, that's how it looks when they're babies," Molly said, though she actually had no idea. She assumed it was normal, however, from what she had seen on television.

"How am I supposed to clean it?" Moss asked.

"With wipes," Molly said. She rooted in the bag until she found a nearly-empty container of baby wipes and handed it to him.

"This is disgusting. I can't believe people willingly have babies," he said. He laid the baby down, took a couple of wipes and swiped them over the baby, smearing everything around.

"You really have to get in there and get her clean," Molly said, mostly because, at the particular moment, she was enjoying his misery. Until now the most difficult, disgusting thing he'd had to deal with in his life was a muddy job site.

He gagged a total of five more times, but he got the baby cleaned up and a new diaper put on. "Now can I put her down?"

"Yes," Molly agreed and watched while he lay the baby in her bassinet. She immediately began to cry.

"Now what's wrong with her?" Moss asked when he returned from washing his hands.

"I think she wants held," Molly said.

"I can't hold her all night," he said. "She's supposed to be sleeping."

"Babies have their days and nights all mixed up in the beginning. They have to learn to sleep at night and not all day," she informed him. She had heard someone say that on a TLC reality show once.

"What am I supposed to do?" he asked, staring at Molly imploringly. He wanted Molly to take the baby, to fix it and make her stop crying. Molly wanted that, too. It broke her heart to hear the newborn's plaintive wails. But Moss was the father; he *had* to do this.

"Pick her up and walk with her, bounce her, talk to her," she said.

"Why? She can't understand anything I'm saying."

"She can understand your tone."

He picked the baby up and she immediately stopped crying.

"See? She loves you already," Molly said.

"What should I say to her?" Moss asked.

"Tell her about yourself," she instructed.

He frowned, but he began to talk as he paced the small living space. "Hi, I'm Moss. I'm your dad, I guess. I'm Italian, and so are you, apparently. Um, we Samperis like to eat. A lot. And we like to argue with each other. A lot. I build houses, and I'm a certified HVAC installer. You have no idea what that means, but it's fairly lucrative and saves us a lot of money hiring outside help. I like music."

"Sing for her," Molly urged.

So he did. He walked in a tight circle, singing and bouncing, until the baby was fast asleep and Molly's heart was completely melted. *"Can I put her down now?"* Moss mouthed.

Molly nodded. They both crept to the bassinet and watched as he put Bella down. She gave a little shuddering sigh and they held their breath until her breathing resumed its deep pace. Moss slid his arm around Molly.

"We did it," he whispered.

"You did it," she whispered, giving his waist a squeeze. "You can totally do this, Moss. I have faith in you."

"Maybe," he whispered with a faint smile. And then the baby woke up and started to scream some more.

CHAPTER 8

It was, hands down, the worst night Molly had ever passed in her life. Bella would only stop crying if she was being held and walked. Eventually, Molly gave up on making Moss try to do it himself and they took turns swapping her back and forth. Eventually, toward daybreak, Bella fell into a deep sleep in her bassinet and Molly and Moss crashed on the couch, each of them taking an end.

Two hours later, when it was time to go to work, they sat groggily at the table eating cereal.

"What are you going to do with her today?" Molly asked.

"I thought you..." he began, but Molly interrupted him with a shake of her head.

"I have to work," Moss continued. "We have that big project to finish at the Rodriguez ranch."

"I know. I work there too, remember?" she said.

He rubbed his eyes. "I don't know what to do with her. I'll have to find someone."

Against her better judgment, she took pity on him. "I'll take her to the office with me, if you swear you will spend your lunch break finding fulltime care for her," she said.

He nodded. "All right."

"And you need to find an apartment," she said.

"I know," he agreed, rubbing his hand wearily over his face. "Can we take your car today? My dad is coming by for his truck. Maybe this weekend I can install some seatbelts in the back of the Mustang."

"We can take my car," she agreed. As for his car, she would leave him to face that nightmare on his own.

They finished breakfast and Molly loaded the dishes in the dishwasher before loading Bella and all of her necessities into the car. She drove to work. Moss dozed, and she envied him. When they arrived at work, Moss hopped into Joe's work truck without a goodbye or backward glance to Molly or Bella.

Molly set Bella's carrier on the floor and got to work as quickly as she could, bracing for the inevitability that Bella would wake and require attention. An hour later, she did. And then, as the night before, she refused to be put down. Molly, who was a soft touch when Moss wasn't around, gave in completely, holding, snuggling, kissing, and caressing the baby while attempting to work one handed. Her productivity was halved, but now that the taxes were done, it wasn't so hectic.

Moss arrived at noon. Molly handed the baby to him and he patted her absently as he sank into a chair and put his feet up.

"Thirty two," he announced.

"What's thirty two?" Molly asked, too tired for clever guesses. And she needed to use the time he was there to try and catch up on her work.

"The number of places I called today looking for a sitter. Of those, only five take newborns. One of the five had three large inside dogs that sounded like they ate babies for snacks. The other four sounded as if they'd just gotten out of prison or were headed there within the week. Mol, I may not be parent of the year, but I swear I can't send her to any of those places. What am I going to do?"

Molly would undoubtedly regret what she was about to say, but the thought of handing Bella over to a shady stranger was immensely painful to her, as well. "I guess I could keep watching her for a bit, until you find a non-murderer to take over. But I'm going to charge you extra." She didn't care about the money so much as forcing him to realize childcare was neither easy nor cheap.

"I'll pay you whatever you want," he told her. "And I'll feel so much better if she's with you. You're the only person outside family I trust anyway. And you're so good with her, so sweet and nurturing." He was giving her the look.

"Are you hitting on me while holding the baby you just had with another woman?" she asked.

"Kind of," he confessed.

"Stop it."

"I'll try, but hitting on women comes naturally to me."

"Apparently," she said, gesturing to the baby.

He sucked in a breath. "Ouch. I have to get back to work."

"How about a kiss?" she suggested. He leaned forward with a pucker, and she put up her hand. "For your child, Moss. But not on the lips because that can spread diseases."

He kissed the baby's head and sniffed. "She kind of stinks."

"I think she needs a bath," Molly said.

"You have to wash them? I sort of hoped they were self-cleaning, like a cat," he said. "She's so tiny. I could drown her or drop her when she's all lathery."

"They make special baths for babies. Does she have one?"

"I don't think so."

"She also needs more diapers, wipes, formula, and clothes," Molly said. "And maybe a bottle and some pacifiers. I'll make a list and we can go after work."

"Thanks, Mol. I owe you."

"Yep," Molly agreed.

He handed her Bella. "How about a kiss?" She kissed the baby. "I meant for me."

"Keep dreaming," she told him.

"Oh, I will. See you after work."

Several hours later, they left the baby store dazed and exhausted. An alert employee noticed their arrival and, seeing their complete cluelessness, loaded them down with everything Moss or Bella might need. They walked away with a stroller, formula, diapers, clothes, bottles, pacifiers, toys, board books, a portable crib, a swing, and a baby wearing system the employee told Molly would change her life.

"It might be a little ouchy, if you had a c-section," she had warned, and Molly didn't bother to tell her she wasn't Bella's mother. What could she say? *It's not my baby, it's my boss's, but he's temporarily staying with me, and I'm taking care of his child, the one he had with a drug addict?* How had her rather simple life turned into such a complicated mess?

For supper, they went to a restaurant. Their waitress asked if they wanted a high chair, and they looked at each other in confusion. "She can't sit up yet," Moss said, and the woman laughed.

"You turn it upside down and put the car seat in it so she doesn't have to be on the floor," the waitress said.

"Oh, ha, ha, sorry. We're kind of sleep deprived," Moss explained.

The woman smiled. "It's okay, I was like that with my first, too. It gets better."

"First?" Moss whispered when she walked away. "Why would anyone do this more than once? And how could anyone afford to?"

They sat and the waitress arranged Bella in the high chair/car seat container for them. "Do you think she'd be willing to lift my arms to open the menu and then order for me?" Moss asked. "I don't think I've ever been this exhausted. And can we talk about the fact that I dropped five hundred dollars at a baby store, something I didn't even know existed a week ago."

"I dozed off at my computer for five minutes today," Molly said.

"I almost fell asleep on a roof beam," Moss replied. "Tell me the truth, Mol. Before yesterday, did you know babies eat every two hours and don't sleep, like, ever?"

"Yes, but there's a vast difference between knowledge and experience," she said.

"You know after I looked for babysitters today, I scrolled over and looked at vasectomy doctors. Apparently I'm too young to get one," he said.

"Moss," Molly exclaimed, alarmed. "You can't make permanent decisions when you're exhausted."

"I probably wouldn't have gone through with it. It made me feel better to think about it," he said. "Don't you ever think about doing crazy things?"

"Yes," she said.

He set down his menu. "Really? Like what? What's crazy for Molly?"

"Letting my boss and his daughter live with me," she said.

"That's right, I am your boss. Sometimes I forget. What can I order you to do for me?" he said.

"How about stay up with you all night passing an eight pound baton and then babysit her all day while I do my regular job for you?"

"No, something really good," he said.

"Lead you out of a forest and back to civilization?" she suggested. "Loan you my car? Run interference for you when some girl you've gone out with calls the office looking for you? Handle all your personal financial information, even though I don't do that for anyone else in the office? Go fish shopping with you when you decide you want a pet and then talk you down off the ledge when you change your mind and want to get a bullmastiff puppy? Drive through Taco Bell for you approximately once a week for the past three years when you forget to take a lunch to work? And then never get repaid for it because you haven't carried money in your wallet since Nixon?"

"No, something better than all that," he said and nudged her foot. "Have you really done all that stuff for me?"

"That was a partial list," she told him.

The waitress came to take their order then. Bella began to stir. Molly got her out of her carrier and held her.

"Why would a girl like you continue to like a guy like me?" he said. "You're beautiful and smart and put together. You could have anyone."

"The golden question," she said.

"I'm serious, Molly. Have you dated anyone in the last three years since you've worked for us?" he asked.

"Now is not the time to discuss my dating life," she told him. Bella began to wriggle in what Molly had already discovered was her hungry squirm. She passed her off to Moss so she could prepare a bottle. "If I ever have a baby of my own, I'm going to do my best to nurse. These bottles and cans of formula are the worst." She took the baby back from Moss who regarded her solemnly.

"It bothers me to think of you having a baby with another man," he admitted.

"Really? Do you think that would be hard, being around someone who had a baby with another person?" she asked as she cuddled Bella close and fed her a bottle.

"Why don't you hate me?" he asked.

"Sometimes I do," Molly said. Their food arrived, saving both of them from further conversation.

CHAPTER 9

Bella had another terrible night. Unlike the night before, Molly and Moss did not work together toward a solution. They turned on each other and began assigning blame.

"You shouldn't have let her sleep so long this evening," Moss accused.

"You could have taken her and kept her awake, but you fell asleep," Molly replied.

"I'm tired," Moss complained.

"So am I," Molly returned.

"Really? Why don't you try standing in the sun all day, framing a barn, and lifting thousand pound girders and then tell me how tired you are," he said.

"Fine, tomorrow I'll go build the building and you can stay in the office all day trying to entertain an eight pound dictator who screams in your face if you're thirty seconds late with her food twelve times a day. Then you can be the one to coax out her gas bubble while she—wait for it—screams incessantly in your face."

"It's your turn to take her. I've already been holding her for two hours," Moss yelled.

"You've been holding her for twenty minutes," Molly said. "And stop yelling at me. I'm not a Samperi. I've slept two hours in the last two days, I have to take a nap."

"My mom had five kids, and I don't remember her complaining about being tired," Moss said.

"Then maybe you can get your mom to do this for you. Oh, wait, she and your dad threw you out," Molly yelled and then, seeing his stricken expression, felt immediately horrible. "I'm sorry, Moss, that was mean. We're both tired, I get that. Let me get that wrap thingy and give it a try." She went to the guest room, which had become ground zero for staging baby things, and tied the wrap like the woman at the baby store taught her. She slipped a wide-awake Bella inside and patted her back, testing the cloth's strength. "It feels comfy."

"Make sure she can breathe. The lady was adamant about that," Moss said.

Molly pushed back the edge of the wrap to expose Bella's face. "She seems to like it. Maybe she'll let me sit down." She sat and, miraculously, Bella didn't fuss. "I think she likes being over my heart. Get one of the pacifiers for me." He retrieved the pacifier. Molly plugged it in Bella's mouth and held it there while Bella sucked furiously, doing her best Maggie Simpson imitation. A minute later, she was asleep.

Moss leaned on Molly's shoulder. "You're magic," he said. A minute later, he was also asleep. Molly checked on Bella once more, made sure she could breathe freely in the wrap and, after settling into a more comfortable position, joined the sleepers and dropped into slumber herself.

She woke four hours later, when Bella began to squirm for a bottle. Molly eased away from Moss, who was still leaning on her shoulder. He usurped her position on the couch, curled into a ball, and resumed sleeping. Molly studied him for a minute, weighing the pros and cons of waking him and making him take a turn with the baby. On the one hand, she wanted to for the sake of fairness. On the other hand, she was already up. Not only that, but she was forming a bond with Bella, learning her smell, sounds, and signals. She could already tell by the twist of her body whether she was hungry, gassy or using the bathroom. And Bella was beginning to respond to her, turning her head to the sound of Molly's voice and quieting as soon as Molly touched her.

*What happens when...*her mind began, but she wouldn't let herself finish the question. Soon Moss and Bella would be out of her apartment. He would find someone to watch her full time, and Molly would forget all about the sweet little bundle who had temporarily occupied her heart. She would forget, wouldn't she? Eventually? Or would it always hurt to see her and know she had been part but not really part of her life? She had no claim to the baby, physically, legally, or otherwise. She was a caregiver, a foster mom without state approval. It was good practice for when she decided to one day foster for real. Yes, she would think of it that way. She was Bella's foster mom, nothing more.

Molly finished feeding the baby, changed her diaper, and put her into one of the sleep bags the eager salesperson insisted they buy. With crossed fingers, she laid Bella in her bassinet and stood back, holding her breath, but Bella was already asleep. Softly, Molly drew a blanket over Moss and tiptoed to bed. She would be able to hear the baby if she cried, the apartment was that tiny. In the meantime, she had two solid hours before she had to wake for work. Never had the possibility of two hours of sleep seemed so precious.

In the morning, she woke feeling slightly refreshed. Six hours of sleep wasn't a lot, but it was leaps and bounds above the two she had gotten the night before. Moss had slept seven, since he hadn't woken for the baby's middle of the night feeding. Molly expected him to feel better when he woke, but he was still cranky.

He sat up frowning and rubbing his eyes like a pouty four year old. "Why'd you wake me?" he asked.

"Work," she said and somehow refrained from adding *obviously.* Why else would she summon his oh-so-charming presence to ruin her morning?

Bella began to cry and Molly rushed around trying to prep her bottle while finishing making the coffee and getting ready for work. "Can you get her?" she asked Moss who made no move to get off the couch.

"I, like, just woke up," he said, yawning and stretching. Molly looked about for a frying pan to toss at his head. Afraid she might miss and hit the baby instead, she refrained.

Lacking the energy or the time to argue, she picked up Bella and slid her into the beloved wrap. "This thing is worth its weight in gold," she muttered to herself as Bella immediately calmed and stared around her with interest.

"It cost so much it might as well be made of gold," Moss said. He stood and went into the bathroom without another word. A second later, Molly heard the shower running.

"I'm going to kill him," she prattled in a cheerful singsong to Bella. "Yes, I am. Don't get used to having a daddy because he's a dead man walking, yes he is." Bella blinked at her and almost seemed to be smiling. Of course babies so tiny couldn't smile. Could they? Molly had no idea. "You like it when I say he's a goner?" she sang, and Bella blinked happily up at her. "They'll never find the body, no they won't," she said, bouncing and patting Bella's behind.

"You look happy this morning," Moss said. Fresh from the shower, his curls straightened out to long tendrils that lay over his eyes. He shoved them away and smiled at her.

"Don't I always look happy?" she asked.

"No. A lot of times you look…worried," he said and then frowned as if realizing the truth of his statement. "Are you worried a lot?"

"Isn't everyone?" she countered.

"No," he said. "Not me."

"Do you think babies this young can smile?" she asked, changing the subject away from herself. She turned her body so Moss could look at Bella's face, but he barely glanced at her on his way to the kitchen.

"No idea," he said. He poured himself a huge mug of coffee, followed by a tub-sized bowl of cereal with milk. "We need more food."

I'll nip right out and buy some as soon as I'm done caring for your child, Molly thought, but she didn't say it because he had already pulled out his phone and started scrolling. When he was finished with his food, he stood and tucked his phone in his pocket.

"Are you ready?" he asked.

"No, I'm not," she snapped. She flew around in a flurry, trying to do the last few things she hadn't been able to do while attending to the baby, and then she rinsed Moss's dishes and stuck them in the dishwasher. Moss was already waiting in her car, keys in hand and sitting in the driver's seat.

"We're going to be late," he said while she strapped Bella in her car seat and double checked the bag to make sure she had everything.

"Why are you driving?" she asked.

"Because I was trying to help us get there on time, but if it's that big of a deal, I can stop the car and we can do a Chinese fire drill and put you in this seat," he snapped. "Geez, Molly."

Molly took a deep breath and glanced back at the baby who was sleeping peacefully. She wouldn't risk waking her with a row, but tonight she and Mossimo Samperi were going to have a very serious chat.

$\mathcal{M}$olly intended to have it out with Moss after work, but Moss didn't come home. She received a text from him late in the afternoon, while she was busy on a work call.

Can you watch the baby tonight I have a thing, was all it said.

Molly read it three times to make sure she wasn't missing anything.

"Anyone have any idea where Moss was going tonight?" she asked his siblings as they filed into the office at the end of the day.

"No idea," Giovanni said. "Though, if I had to guess, I would say it involves a circus and probably some cotton candy."

"You're a saint, Molly. None of the rest of us are willing to put up with him, and I've never seen my dad this mad before," Jessamine said.

"Don't let him run over you," Benny advised. "Because we all know he will, if you let him."

"He's a spoiled brat," Joe added. "I love him, but I also want to kill him."

Molly swallowed hard at the look of deep pain etched on his face. Of all of them, Moss's rash actions had had the most effect on Joe and Peaches. Though Joe hadn't said it in words, his drawn features told them all that things had been bad at home since the news of Bella broke.

Where are you? Molly texted Moss, but there was no answer.

She gathered Bella and went home, fixing a bottle for the baby and trying to eat a salad for herself whenever time permitted. Bella was fussy and gassy and no amount of bouncing or patting seemed to make a difference. And Molly had been on baby duty endlessly since the night before. "And it's not even my baby," she said to herself. "You're adorable, Bella, but why am I doing this?" Bella's only answer was to scream as another gas bubble hit her. She writhed in Molly's arms, and the only thing that worked to calm her was walking in endless circles, bouncing deeply while patting her back. It required all of Molly's coordination, focus, and energy, and she was already running on empty.

Eventually the baby settled down. Molly fed her, changed her, and put her in the bassinet. All of the crying must have worn her out because she slept soundly. Molly checked the clock; it was midnight. She should also be sleeping, but she was too angry.

The door was locked, but Moss let himself in shortly after midnight. "You had a key made," she said when he walked through the door.

"I didn't think you'd mind," he said. She stood, walked closer, and sniffed him.

"You went to *Truckers*," she said.

"I was auditioning a new band," he explained.

"Out," she said.

"What?" he asked, frowning in confusion.

"Out, get out of my apartment. Take your stuff but leave the baby, I care about her too much to have her dragged out of here by you in the middle of the night. You can get her tomorrow, or maybe I'll call Children's Services to have her placed somewhere else, with a responsible family."

He held perfectly still, waiting for the punch line. Instead, she opened the door and began tossing his stuff outside.

"Wait, Molly, what are you doing?" he asked.

"That's a great question, Moss, a really great question. What am I doing? Why am I killing myself to take care of your child? Why am I letting you live with me, rent free? Why am I cleaning up after you like you're a toddler? Why have I been bending over backwards to help you out when you are too spoiled and immature to even appreciate it or say thank you?"

"Is that what this is about? You want rent and for me to say thank you?" he said.

"You don't get it, you never get it." She spoke slowly, punctuating her words so he couldn't fail to hear them. "You don't get to be a child when you have a child. You can't go to bars and try to be the star of your own rock band anymore. You can't invest all your time and money in a stupid car that doesn't even have seatbelts. You can't leave your baby for hours on end with your secretary. What is wrong with you? Seriously, Moss, I've asked myself this question for years, and now I'm asking you. What is wrong with you?" She was yelling, and she tried to calm down. Not because she wanted to, but because she didn't want one of her neighbors to call the police.

Moss sank to the couch. "I don't know, Molly. I really don't know. I think I might be seriously messed up."

"You know what? So am I, so is everybody. But it doesn't stop us from getting it together and functioning, especially when you have a child in the mix. Your daughter does not deserve to have a dad who does anything less than make her the center of his universe."

"You're right, okay? You're right." He started to cry then, with large, fat tears running down his cheeks unchecked. "I'm a screw up, and I want to do better, but I don't know how to do better. Everyone is always telling me to grow up, but no one ever tells me how. I literally don't know what to do to make things better, and I don't know how. I need, like, some kind of manual for real life or something."

Molly sat beside him, on the couch but far away and not touching. "Do you really mean that?"

He nodded and wiped his face on his sleeve.

"Because I can tell you how to be a grownup, Moss. I can tell you the exact steps to take to get there, but you have to do the work. You have to be an actual adult with me, and you have to be a real parent to your child."

He nodded again. "Just tell me what to do, and I'll do it."

Molly blew out a breath. "I'm going to help you, but this is it for us, Moss, the last straw. If you fail me again, if you fail Bella, then you are out of my life. And I don't just mean out of my apartment and no longer my friend. I mean I will quit my job and move away from here, and you will never see me again. And I never, ever make idle threats. Do you understand? Are we clear?"

He nodded, looking glum and somber. "So, what do I need to do first?"

She reached for a piece of paper and a pen. "Step one is to get your finances in order so you can get an apartment. How much do you have in savings?"

"I don't know, maybe like a few hundred dollars," he said.

She put down the pen and looked at him. "How can that be?" She knew exactly how much he made, and it was almost exactly twice what she made. And she had more than ten thousand dollars in the bank.

"I don't know. Money comes in, money goes out. I never paid much attention."

"But you didn't even have rent or have to pay for food at your parents," she said.

"Are you trying to make me feel worse? I'm a loser in every way, I get it, okay? How do I fix it?" he said.

"You need to start a separate account, something you never see or touch, an emergency savings account. You can get online and set one up through your bank," she said.

"Um, I don't know which bank I use," he said.

It took effort, but she refrained from rolling her eyes. "Lucky for you, your secretary does. And she knows your bank account and routing numbers."

"Have you been stealing from me?" he said.

"Yes, Moss. I've been embezzling those cobwebs from your

account," she said. She pulled her laptop close and began typing furiously. A few minutes later, she closed it again. "There. You're putting five hundred a month in the new account, and you can't touch it without a fourteen day advanced notice."

"What's next? Help me, Obi Wan, you're my only hope," he said.

"Next I go to bed because I'm exhausted. And if your baby cries tonight, you get up with her, give her a bottle, burp her, and change her."

"What if she won't stop crying?" he asked.

"We'll cross that bridge if we get there, but don't panic. You already know how to feed, burp, and change her. Nothing new there. She really likes her sleep sack; I think she might have been cold before. Make sure her tummy is full and she's snuggly warm and safe."

"You make it sound and look so easy, Mol," he said. "Thank you." He closed the distance between them and kissed her cheek.

She touched his cheek and gave it a pat. "Hold on to that sentiment. The real work starts tomorrow."

"Can I ask you a question before you go?" he said.

"What's that?"

"You said every daughter wants to be the center of her dad's universe. Is that how it is with you and your dad? I've never heard you mention him."

She looked away. "I don't have a dad."

"Everyone has a dad."

"I suppose I had one, but he left when I was a baby. I never knew him," she said.

"I'm sorry," he said, squeezing her hand. She squeezed his in return.

"I know what it is to grow up without a dad, Moss. Don't let it happen to Bella."

"I won't," he promised. "I'm going to fix this."

"I have faith in you. I think," she said, tweaking his knuckle. She stood and, after an irresistible tousle of his curls, went to her room and closed the door.

On the couch, Moss lay awake for a long time, thoughts of Molly and Bella mashing together in his brain. Somehow they felt interconnected, like if he let down one of them, he would be letting down both of them. He had no idea how to proceed, but he knew he had to try because, though he had known one for three years and one for three days, he couldn't stand to lose either.

CHAPTER 11

The next morning Molly woke and went out to the living room where Moss stood wearing a clumsy wrap with the baby inside. She went forward and repositioned some things, giving both Moss and the baby a pat.

"Fatherhood looks good on you," she said.

"I'm exhausted," he replied.

"The good kind of exhausted?" she asked.

"Is there a good kind?" he said, but he was smiling.

"Do you want me to take her for a while so you can shower?"

"Yes, please," he said and, with effort, pulled the baby out of the wrap and handed her to Molly. "And thank you," he added, kissing Molly's cheek as he handed the baby over.

"You're welcome," Molly replied. She had heard him get up in the night with the baby, but it didn't seem to last long and she had felt no need to come to his rescue. After a—nearly—full night of sleep, she almost felt like herself again.

She sat at the table, holding the baby and eating her cereal one handed while scrolling through a notebook.

"What's that?" Moss asked after he emerged fresh-faced and wet-haired from the shower.

This is the manual you requested. I've been jotting things as I've thought of them."

"It's huge," he exclaimed.

"I've been thinking about that, too. I think we should try one new thing a day instead of instituting too many changes at one time," she said.

"Whatever you say, teach," he said.

She had two months to try and turn him into a functioning adult before his mother got her claws back into him. Could she do it? At some point his enthusiasm for the project would wane. He would hit the wall and want to quit. That would be the real test, whether he pushed through and persevered or gave up and reverted to old ways.

"Yesterday you opened a savings account, and that was pretty easy, right?"

"Painless," he agreed.

"And you already have a job, so you're leaps and bounds ahead of the pack there," she said.

"And I always show up for work on time," he added helpfully.

"That's right, you do have a rock solid work ethic. How did that happen?" she asked.

"My dad."

"What else did your dad teach you?"

"Everything I know about construction, plus don't hit girls, even your sister when she's being the most annoying person on the planet," he said. He finished his giant bowl of cereal and pushed it to the center of the table, presumably to wait for the magic dish fairies to take it away.

"Today I thought we could work on something called 'picking up after yourself.' This includes putting away your clothes, picking up your wet towel off the bathroom floor, and rinsing your dishes and putting them into the dishwasher. Basically, you put away anything you get out or use."

He raised his hand.

"Yes, a question down front," she said.

"I don't know how to load a dishwasher," he said.

"Lucky for you, I'm not type-A about that kind of stuff. As long as the dish goes in and doesn't block the spinny thingy, we're good."

"Good because one time I tried to put a dish into Giovanni and Vivian's dishwasher, and they freaked out like it was the apocalypse because I didn't know their system."

"That's because Giovanni and Vivian are both so uptight it's a surprise they don't squeak when they walk," Molly said.

Moss gasped. "I'm going to tell them you said that."

"And I'll tell them you're lying. Who do you think they'll believe?" she batted her eyes at him and aimed for an innocent expression.

"You're chillingly diabolical. I love it," he said. He stood, rinsed his dish, and placed it into the dishwasher. "Now I'm going to pick up my clothes from the bathroom. Question: where does the wet towel go after it comes off the floor?"

"There's a hook on the back of the door," she told him.

"Don't you use a new towel every day?" he asked.

"Sure, if you want to wash seven towels a week. I try to get a few uses out of each towel so I save a little money on laundry."

He stopped short. "What does money have to do with laundry?"

"I don't have a washer or a dryer, so I have to pay money to use them," she explained.

"So that's what Laundromats are for," he said, tapping his temple.

"Soon the student will surpass the master," she said.

He finished picking up and carried the baby to the car. He had never strapped the baby in before, so Molly showed him how to do it.

"That's two new things for today. I am well over my limit," he said.

"I've decided you're gifted and can occasionally handle more work than the other kids," she said. They arrived at work happy and smiling. Moss carried the baby inside, took her out of her car seat, and kissed her goodbye before handing her to Molly.

She smiled approvingly. "Have a good day, Bob the Builder."

"Thank you," he said.

Molly sat down, feeling more at ease and peaceful than she had in days. "I think your dad might actually love you," she told Bella who regarded her with a few serious blinks. For Molly, it felt like she was helping to right a wrong. Maybe if she could fix the relationship between Moss and his daughter, it would save Bella from all the pain Molly had gone through in her life. This was what she had always wanted, to help kids like her. In a way, Moss was helping her fulfill one of her life's goals.

In the afternoon, Jessamine stopped by to pick up a client portfolio. She caught sight of Bella and crept tentatively closer. "I haven't had the heart to look at her yet, in case it turns out to all be a big mistake," Jessamine explained. She peeked over the blanket and gasped. "She's really his, isn't she? It's like looking at Moss when he was a baby."

"She's really his," Molly said.

"Can I hold her?" Jessamine asked.

"Of course," Molly said and handed her over.

"My first niece," she said, her eyes going teary. "This could have been amazing. Why did Moss have to screw it up for all of us?"

Molly shrugged, not knowing what to say.

"She's so precious," Jessamine continued. She snuggled the baby closer under her chin. "Your aunt Jess is so going to spoil you to pieces." For the better part of the next hour, Jessamine held, cuddled, and fed the baby while Molly caught up on her work.

"I have to give her back," she reluctantly said. "I have a client meeting. But I'm definitely going to have to spend more time in the office. My blood pressure feels miraculously lower."

"It's like petting a cat that screams a lot," Molly said.

Jessamine laughed and then tilted her head at her. "Is this weird for you? Moss is staying with you and you're taking care of his baby round the clock. You can tell him to shove it, none of us would think less of you."

"It's fine," Molly said. "I'm enjoying her."

"She's highly enjoyable," Jess said, giving the baby another pat before grabbing her things and heading out.

The rest of the day went smoothly for both Molly and Bella. Things felt like they were beginning to gel, as if they were slipping into a routine that kept Bella content and allowed Molly to get her work done. Mostly, she liked being in the wrap, snuggled next to Molly's body as much as possible. Beyond that she only required feeding, changing, and the occasional patting and bouncing out of a gas bubble.

Moss picked up Molly at the end of the day, and they went grocery shopping. "Where do you want to go for supper?" he asked after they left the store.

"We just spent a hundred bucks on groceries," she reminded him. "I was going to cook."

"I didn't know you could cook," he said.

"I can't say I'm awesome at it, but I do it. It's a lot cheaper than eating out all the time. Plus fewer calories."

"I'd say you're doing fine in the calorie department," he said, eyeing her body with appreciation.

She shook her head.

"What? I'm not allowed to give you compliments?" he asked.

"Yes, but you need to run them through a filter first. If it's something you could say when you're a ninety-year-old guy and not sound creepy, then it's okay. If it would someday make you sound like the kind of person whose picture would appear in a preschool with a giant warning label, then no," she said.

"You're pretty," he tried.

"Yes, that's nice and not at all creepy," she agreed.

"And your body is smoking hot," he added.

"Why'd you have to go and ruin it?" she asked. "Think Carey Grant, not Justin Bieber. Keep it classy."

"I'm still not sure I get it," he said.

"Think of Bella. Would you want some guy drooling all over her and telling her she's a hot piece of tail?" she asked.

"You want me to treat you like you're my daughter?" he said with a grimace.

"I want you to treat me like I'm someone's daughter," she said.

"Huh," he said, sitting back with what she knew was his deep-thinking expression.

He held Bella while Molly made supper. They ate in comfortable silence, and he helped her clean up without being asked. When that was finished, they sat on the couch and scanned for anything on television.

"Can I ask you a serious question?" Moss said after a while.

"Shoot," Molly replied.

"Is this all there is? Is this my life now? Before, I was hardly ever home. I went out with my friends or played with my band. And now I'm sitting on your couch watching *Frontline*. I'm twenty five, and I don't feel ready for retirement yet, you know? No offense because you know I like you, but this is boring. If this is being a grownup, why does anyone want to grow up?"

Molly muted the television.

"I hurt your feelings, didn't I? I'm sorry."

"You didn't," Molly assured him. "I'm glad you're being honest. I'd rather you get it all out rather than let it build up and explode. I guess I would answer your question with a question. Did you feel fulfilled? Because you told me before our date you were ready for a change."

"Did I feel fulfilled?" he mused. "Not really, but I had a lot of fun. I didn't feel all these pressures weighing me down. I'm starting to get why you look worried all the time, by the way."

"I would suggest to you that everyone has to grow up sometime. Even your super cool friends who hang out in the bar every night will get their comeuppance one day. Usually it happens gradually, like a shedding of skin. You start outgrowing stuff until eventually the old things that brought you joy no longer do. Your problem is that your comeuppance has come like a brick wall. You're having to drop everything all at once and make drastic life changes. I get it, Moss, it's not easy. I guess it's up to you to decide if it's worth it."

"I'm twenty five, and I see my life stretching out before me in small increments of washing bottles and not sleeping," he said.

"I know," she soothed. "It's a lot, but she's an infant. Babies require a crazy amount of work and time and effort. It will get easier. You'll get into a groove that will begin to feel normal, and you'll start finding time to go out and do stuff with your friends. It's not always going to be this hard."

He took her hand and gave it a squeeze. "Why are you so good at adulting? We're the same age."

"I've had a lot of practice," she told him.

"Why?" he said. "What's your story, Mol? Because I'd rather hear it than watch one more minute of educational television. You said you're from here, but we didn't go to high school together. Were you homeschooled?"

"No. I lived in Ansonia, with my grandmother. My mom has issues."

He squinted, thinking hard. "But I remember when we hired you Joe said you were from Portland. I thought that was cool, and I forgot about it until just now, probably because you have a local accent."

"When I was twelve, my mom came to claim me from my grandma and dragged me to Portland."

"And that didn't go well," he deduced from her tone.

"It went very, very not well. We ended up on the street. Homelessness is pretty common there, so we stayed in a lot of shelters and I was able to continue going to school. I got a job at a fast food restaurant and saved enough money for bus fare to get back here."

"And then what happened?" he prodded, sensing he would have to drag her story from her.

"My grandma had died, while I was in Portland. So I was homeless again. A girl I had gone to school with took pity on me and let me use her address so I could get another job, fast food again. I did so well they gave me a scholarship, and I put myself through community college. Then, when I graduated, I took a job with Samperi Builders. The end."

"And now you're taking care of a pampered rich kid who doesn't know how to load a dishwasher," he said. "What do you see in me?"

"A whole lot of potential," she said. A buzz of electricity zapped between them. Bella began to fuss, breaking the spell. "I'll feed her, and then I'm going to go to bed."

"I'll feed her," he said. "Hey, so I know, what's on tomorrow's agenda in my How To Be A Grownup Manual?"

"Finding an apartment," she said.

"Oh, right, that," he said. His gaze slid around the tiny living room. "The coziness of this place has grown on me."

Molly smiled. "See, being a peasant isn't so bad."

"It's all about who you're doing it with, and I've got a good crew here," Moss said. He picked up Bella and kissed her, and Molly felt her heart ping.

"Right," she agreed. "I'll listen for the baby and take the night shift. I know you're tired."

"You don't have to," Moss said.

"People who are appreciated will always do more than what's expected," she informed him.

"I feel like I've heard that somewhere before," he said.

"I'm thinking of getting it tattooed on my bicep," she said. She kissed Bella's head, patted Moss's cheek, and went to bed.

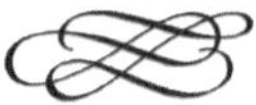

CHAPTER 12

The next morning, Moss was up before Molly. He had already fed and changed Bella and set out Molly's cereal bowl and spoon.

"This is like having Alice from the *Brady Bunch*," Molly said. "Thank you."

"I was thinking," Moss began, "about apartments. What if, instead of moving out and getting my own place, I stay here instead?"

"Um," Molly said. A Cheerio lodged in her throat and she coughed until a sip of coffee dislodged it.

"Hear me out, okay? I'm not suggesting I continue to sponge off you. But Bella is happy and settled here. Moving would mean uprooting her out of her routine and comfort zone. And you do have a spare room. What if I bought a bed and moved Bella's stuff in there with me? And I would pay you rent because I know how you feel about pretty, pretty money."

"It pays the bills," she agreed. "But I have concerns."

"What concerns?" he asked.

"You're my boss. Is it weird if we're also roommates? I mean, how does that even work?" she said.

"Exactly as it has been working. And if it stops working, I'll move out," he said. He raised his hand as if taking an oath. "I promise I'll be good. I'll help keep things clean and help share the cost of food. You won't even know I'm here, except for the dirty diapers. And Bella promises to try and keep them to a minimum."

"I guess we could keep it going on a continued trial basis." She glanced at her list. "Maybe we should skip over finding an apartment and move on to finding a suitable car."

He dropped his spoon. "Please don't tell me you're going to make me give up the Love Machine."

"You're a grown man, Moss, I can't make you do anything."

He gave her a look.

"Okay, I won't make you. Maybe it can be your weekend sometimes fun car, but you do need to find a suitable vehicle that can accommodate Bella's car seat."

"This is awkward, but I have to ask," he said, twisting his napkin to shreds. "I've never had to worry about my finances before. Can I afford a new car?"

"Let's look," she said. She took her laptop from its bag and brought up his account. "This is what you make each pay, and this is how much you have in the bank."

"What?" he yelled, startling Bella who began to cry. "How can I possibly make that much and have nothing to show for it?"

"That's a whole other can of worms. Let's focus on the vehicle. Out of this net pay..."

"What's net?" he interrupted.

"Gross pay is what you make before taxes." She showed him his gross pay. "Net is what you make after everything has been deducted."

"They take out that much in taxes? Oh, I am definitely going to vote in the next election. Make a note to tell me how to register to vote and where to go to vote and also how to use a voting machine."

"Focus," she reminded him. "Out of your net, you're setting aside five hundred for emergencies. That leaves you with this much."

"That seems like enough for a decent car," he said.

"Wait, you haven't accounted for rent, utilities, gas, insurance, groceries, your phone, childcare, diapers, formula, car upkeep, toiletries, and a bit for miscellaneous items." She wrote a number beside each thing she jotted down, added it up, and gave him the total. "This is about what you have to spend on a car."

His face was crestfallen. "I'm going to have to get a clunker, aren't I?"

"That's for you to decide. I deal in numbers," she said.

"How does anyone make it on so little?" he asked.

Molly couldn't help it, she laughed out loud. "Moss, do you have any idea how much I make?"

"You don't make the same as me?" he said.

"This is my monthly net," she said and wrote down the number for him.

His jaw dropped. "How are you still alive?"

"I'm careful because I have to be," she said. "And it's also more money than I've ever made in my life, so it seems like a lot to me. When you come from nothing, you appreciate everything."

"I guess the opposite must be true too, huh?" he mused. He checked his phone. "We should go."

"Definitely," she agreed. Tossing down the rest of her coffee, she double checked Bella's bag while Moss buckled the baby into her car seat and picked up the carrier.

"Ready, Roomie?" he asked.

"Ready," she agreed, and they headed off to work together.

That day Giovanni stopped into the office on the pretense he'd forgotten something. Everyone knew Giovanni never forgot anything, however. He was Mr. Prepared and the person Moss had to ask when he ran out of something on a jobsite. He was only three years older than Molly and Moss, but she thought of him on the same level as Joe and Benny—old and settled. The fact that he had eloped on a first date was still hard to believe, though when she met Vivian it got easier to envision. He and Vivian were two halves of a whole, both quiet, conservative, and intellectual.

Molly watched as he paced through the office a couple of times and then stopped at her desk and picked up the candy jar. He didn't like the chocolate mints she kept out for Moss. He rarely ate candy, but when he did, he preferred coffee drops. Molly retrieved them from her desk drawer and handed them over.

"Thanks," he said, taking a couple and opening one. He fidgeted for a while longer, out of excuses.

"Do you want to hold the baby?" Molly asked, deciding to put him out of his misery.

"Yes, but I've never actually held a baby," he said. "Except Moss, and I'm pretty sure I dropped him on his head a few times, if his current behavior is any indication."

"It's really easy. Do you want to sit down?"

"Maybe I'd better," Giovanni said. He sat and straightened his perfectly crisp chinos so the lines ran parallel to each other. He cleared his throat and held out his arms. Molly placed the baby into them and repositioned him so he was supporting her head and bottom.

"Oh, wow," he said, a little breathless. "She's so tiny." Unlike Jessamine, he didn't coo at her or sing or even talk to her. He stared unblinking as if trying to process the new information and memorize her face. Then, after about half an hour of perfect silence, he gave her back. It seemed like a cold reception for such a tiny infant, but Molly had spent three years making a study of the Samperis. She knew, therefore, that Giovanni was deeply moved and had probably gone off somewhere alone to think or categorize the newfound feelings for his niece.

In normal circumstances, Joe probably would have been the first to embrace Bella. But her life was a painful reminder of his lack, and it would probably be a while. For Molly, Benny was the surprise holdout.

"He feels conflicted," Lou told Molly when she showed up for their weekly lunch. "He wants to support Moss, but he also feels solidarity with Joe. I think once Joe finally cracks and sees the baby, Benny will be all over it. He already bought her a toy, handmade by Costa Rican refugees and sold at the free trade store, because of course. I bought her a savings bond because, in about a decade, it will be the gift that keeps on giving."

An hour before closing time, as Molly was feeding Bella her bottle, the door opened and a man walked in. Walk-ins were rather unusual but not completely out of the question.

"Hi, can I help you?" Molly asked. The man looked vaguely familiar, but she couldn't place him.

"Hey, it's you," he said.

"It's me?" she said.

"You were at *Truckers* a few months ago. I tried to buy you a drink, and you shot me down cold. You said you were with someone. I guess you really meant it," he said, gesturing to Bella.

"She's not mine," Molly blurted. "She's my…I'm her babysitter."

His gaze slid around the construction office. "You're a real multitasker."

"You should see me juggle," she said. When he smiled, she remembered him. He had been the guy with such a pleasant smile that he exuded friendliness, and the smile had the same effect today. "Can I help you, or do you go around tracking women who refused your drink offers?"

"Busted, but I'm also here on business." He pulled out his briefcase and laptop and began laying out for her exactly what he needed built, a storefront for a sporting goods company he worked for.

"I can tell you the Samperis are super busy right now. They're finishing one big project and getting ready to launch another," she said.

"The TV show?" he guessed.

She put her finger to her lips. "Shh, it's a secret. I will pass this information along to them, though, and get back to you with an answer in the next three days."

"Are you trying to tell me I'll have a concrete answer from a contractor within three days?" he said.

"It's the Samperi way," she told him.

"It's witchcraft is what it is," he said. "But I'm not complaining. Here's my card."

She read the card out loud. "'Calvin James.' The final decision is going to rest with the Samperis, but I have to tell you that I don't trust people with two first names."

"I can't catch a break with you, Miss…"

"Molly O'Ryan," she supplied.

"You realize that your name is comprised of two first names," he said.

"Why do you think I have trust issues?" she asked and was rewarded when he laughed.

"Well, Molly O'Ryan, I am definitely glad I stopped in person instead of calling on the phone because now I know where to score a qualified babysitter for my sister's kid. She's always on the lookout," he said.

"Good luck, I don't come cheap," she said.

"I could tell that by looking at you," he said. He closed his briefcase with a click and, with another smile, walked out of the office.

Molly sat back feeling a little confused by the encounter because she had liked him. He was the first guy since she met Moss three years ago who had pinged on her radar, and yet she was closer to Moss than she had ever been. What was happening to her? She shook her head. Nothing was happening to her. She and Moss were roommates and nothing more. It was perfectly acceptable for her to be interested in someone else because she was free, totally and completely free.

As if thinking of Moss had summoned him, he opened the door and walked inside. "There are my girls. Ready to go home?"

"Yes, let me drop this stuff on Joe's desk."

"Calvin James," Moss said, spying the card. "I went to school with him."

"Really? What was he like?" Molly asked.

"Nice, smart, kind of quiet. Not a partier, so we didn't spend a lot of quality time together," he said.

"He needs a storefront for some sporting goods company he works for," Molly said.

"That's his family's company, he didn't mention?" Moss said.

"No, he didn't," Molly said, pleased with the omission. Humility ranked high on her list of desired qualities. Her mind conjured Calvin and his warm smile, and then she saw Moss pick up Bella and kiss her gently on both cheeks, and all other thoughts flitted away.

CHAPTER 13

"Guess what I did today," Moss said, sounding extraordinarily pleased with himself.

"What?" Molly asked.

"I bought a bed and a mattress, all by myself. It's being delivered tonight," he said. "Look, no strings, I'm a real boy."

"Good for you, that's great," Molly said, patting his knee.

"I know this is short notice, but I have to ask you a question." He took her hand. "Molly O'Ryan, will you assemble my bed with me tonight?"

She put her free hand to her chest. "This is so sudden but, yes, a thousand times yes."

He kissed her hand and let it go. "This must be what living the dream feels like," he said. He was being sarcastic, but for Molly, who'd had so little normalcy and stability in her life, it was a dream come true.

"Speaking of which, as I once again used my credit card today and it started smoking from overuse, it occurred to me that I don't actually know how to pay my bills," he said.

"I think your mom set up auto-pay on everything, but we'll look into it tonight and make sure," she said.

"Hey, what should we do for supper?" he asked.

"I was going to cook," she said.

"Again?" he said, sounding disappointed.

"Is my cooking that bad?" she asked.

"No, it's just that I like to eat out," he said.

"I hate to bring you down after the whole grown up bed high you had going, but it's nine days until you get paid," she said. "Unless you want to put everything on credit, you have about a hundred bucks to last until then."

He was quiet for a long time, blinking fast and staring straight ahead. "Well, that sucks," he said at last.

Molly wondered what it would be like to be twenty five and worrying about money for the first time. She had never *not* worried about money. Even as a little kid living within the relative stability of her grandmother's house, she had wondered some days where her food would come from. There had been many times she had gone without lunch at school, laughingly telling people it was because she was on a diet when the truth was that there hadn't been enough food to spare.

"I know why I'm quiet, why are you quiet?" he asked.

"Just thinking," she said.

"Let me guess; I'm getting pretty good at this. You're thinking how were you so lucky to attract a catch like me, an impoverished single parent who is dependent on you for my very survival," he said.

"That is, like, word for word what I was thinking. How did you do that? Spooky," she said.

"I have a secret that might change your mind," he said. "Something almost no one knows about me."

"This isn't your first baby? You're wanted for murder?" she guessed.

"Close. I know how to cook, and I'm pretty awesome at it," he said.

Her jaw dropped. "Are you even joking with me right now? Because it's cruel to tease."

"I will make you a meal tonight, and it will be so good, you will weep and want to take back every mean thing you've ever said about me," he said.

"I don't think I've ever said any mean things about you," she said.

"Oh, then you'll probably just enjoy it and be impressed," he said, and he was right. He made spaghetti, but the sauce was from scratch, and it was amazing.

"Moss, this is seriously the best spaghetti I've ever had," she said.

"I know," he agreed. His phone chirped with a text. He took it out and began to scroll.

"Do you want to do the dishes or feed the baby?" she asked. For a second she feared he wouldn't answer, his nose was still in his phone.

"Baby," he said at last, and tucked his phone in his pocket.

Molly cleaned the kitchen while Moss fed the baby and then they carried his new bedframe into the spare room.

"Here are the instructions," Molly said after they opened the box.

"Instructions? Molly, Molly, Molly, I literally build things for a living. I think I can handle a simple little bed," he said.

Ninety minutes later, when parts were strewn all over the room, he reached for the instructions. "I'm only reading these to make you feel better. I could totally do this on my own," he said. Twenty minutes after he read the instructions, the bed was together. Molly helped him put the mattress and box springs on.

"Did you buy sheets?" she asked.

"Sheets," he said, smacking himself in the head. "I'm like the guy who can catch the ball but can't carry it over the line."

"No worries. Your bed is a different size than mine, but I have an extra set you can make due with until you get some that fit." She went to her room to retrieve them and helped spread them on.

Moss smoothed his hand over the sheets. "Want to test it out?" he asked. He lay sideways across the bed and gave the mattress a pat.

"Definitely," Molly agreed. She picked up Bella and lay her beside Moss. "What do you think of Daddy's new bed, Bells?"

"That is exactly what I meant," Moss said. "It's like you read my mind."

Molly laughed and crawled up on Bella's other side, stretching and yawning. Moss was staring at Bella, his finger tracing the perfect outline of her face.

"Sometimes it hurts to look at her," he said.

"Moss, why?" Molly asked.

"Because I know how much I've already failed her. Babies are supposed to be conceived in love, and I'm not sure I could pick her mother out of a lineup. You said little girls adore their dads, but some day I'm going to have to tell her the truth about my part in how she got here. How could she possibly not think less of me?"

"Moss, my dad walked out on me. Abandoning your kid is one of the worst things you can do to her, but I never, ever stopped wanting him to walk back in again. I used to have this dream that he would come find me in Portland and rescue me. Girls never stop loving and wanting and needing their dads. If you love her, and care for her, and show up daily in her life, she's going to believe you're the best man who has ever lived. And if you turn out to be half the father I know you can be, she'll be right. An awkward conversation about past misdeeds won't do anything to change being a good dad all the other days you're going to have with her."

His hand shifted from Bella to Molly and began gently sifting the hair away from her face. "It's hard to look at you, too, Molly, because I know you've been disappointed in me."

"I'm a big believer in redemption," she told him.

"Haven't you ever made a huge mistake in the heat of the moment, lost control and done something you regretted?" he asked.

"Yes, but probably not what you're talking about," she said.

"No lost weekend with some guy?" he said. "Come on, this is a safe space to confess."

She smiled. "Moss, I'm a virgin."

"What?" he exclaimed so loudly that Bella's startle reflex kicked in and her arms flew out to her sides. He laid his hand on the baby's chest. "Are you joking?" he added in a whisper.

"I'm not joking," she said.

"How is that even possible?" he asked.

"You mean biologically?" she said.

"No, I mean, Molly, you are everything. You are the total package. How have you made it to twenty five without...you know."

"When I was living in the shelters in Portland, sex was currency. You could use it to get food, supplies, drugs, money. But I saw what it did to the women who used it that way, and I vowed never to end up like that. So I went the other extreme and wouldn't even get close. And it's not like I had a lot of free time, what with trying to stay alive, put myself through school, and work."

"Wow," Moss said, "wow."

"You're staring at me like I'm a freak," she said.

"I'm staring at you like you're precious, and now I feel even worse about everything."

"My virginity isn't a weapon I use against people to shame them for their life choices," she said.

"Maybe it should be. Weaponized virginity could be a whole new branch for the military. No one would ever see it coming, that's for sure," he said. "Quick question, can I call you the Virginator?"

"Not if you ever expect me to answer," she said. "And I would prefer not to have this broadcast to the rest of your family."

"I can keep a secret," he said. She gave him a look. "Starting now. It's a moot point anyway, I'm not actually on speaking terms with my family."

"That's only temporary," she assured him.

"I don't get it. I've messed up a million times before and they've never batted a lash. Then you bring home one illegitimate child, and everybody loses their minds."

"Why do you think that might be?" she asked.

"I guess because now my life choices are affecting someone else," he said, his tone rote. "Thank you, teacher, for making me figure it out on my own."

"That's what a good teacher does," she said.

They shared a smile across Bella. His hand continued its slow, soothing work in her hair. "I keep thinking where I would be right now without you, and all I can come up with is either on my friend Dave's couch, along with last week's pizza boxes, or running up enormous bills on my credit card at some hotel. I guess it's true what they say about finding out who your true friends are when things are down."

"You would have done the same for me," she said.

"No, I wouldn't, and we both know it. I probably would have tossed a hundred bucks at you and told you good luck. I wouldn't have gone out of my way for you; I wouldn't have rearranged my life to make sure you were okay."

"Maybe you can pay it forward. Next time somebody is down on his luck, you can be the guy who helps him back up," she said.

"See, that's the thing, I probably would have done all that for one of my buddies. But you've always sort of been there," he said.

"You don't have to keep saying things out loud," she told him. "There's this mechanism in your head that has the ability to stop hurtful words from coming out of your mouth."

"This is me trying to apologize, albeit badly. I'm sorry I didn't pay more attention to you the last few years. I'm sorry I didn't value you the way I should have. I took your interest in me for granted, and I didn't see the very real friendship you were busy providing me, especially when I was at my most unlovable."

"Thank you for the apology. And, for the record, this is not me pursuing you. This is me being a friend, no strings."

"But now I want strings," he said.

"Too late, strings are off the table," she said.

"We'll see," he said, smiling his most charming Moss smile, the one that said he knew he was irresistibly good looking.

Between them, Bella began to squirm for her bottle. "I need to feed her," Molly said.

"She's not crying yet," Moss said.

"If you wait until she cries, then you've waited too long and she's harder to calm down. You have to catch her on the upswing of hunger and not the peak."

"How do you know these things?" he asked.

"I don't know. Maybe instinct, or maybe so much time spent with her." She paused. "Calvin thought she was mine."

"Who?" Moss said. He had already pulled out his phone and started to scroll.

"Calvin James. He thought she was mine when he came into the office."

"Ha, that's funny," Moss said. "You might as well tell people she is, you're doing the mom's job."

Molly carried Bella into the kitchen for her bottle, frowning. She was doing the mom's job, but she was definitely not the mom. She had no rights or benefits beyond that of a caregiver. And every day she got a little more attached. The question wasn't what was she going to do about it, but rather what could she do about it? And the answer was absolutely nothing.

CHAPTER 14

"What's on today's agenda?" Moss asked. As he had the day before, he had already fed Bella and arranged Molly's cereal bowl and spoon on the table for her. It was a small thing, but for Molly, who had spent so many years taking care of herself, it meant a lot.

"Laundry," she said.

"Great, I like a little starch in my collars, and if you could have it back by five, that would be awesome," Moss said. Then, "Ha, ha, see, I can joke about my self-centered incompetence."

"The funniest part is trying to figure out if you mean it," Molly said.

"Doing laundry is totally not rock-n-roll," Moss said.

"Neither is re-using the same pair of underwear for a week," Molly said.

"Depends on the band," Moss replied, and she smiled.

They had fallen into a routine in the short amount of time they had been roommates. Without words, they alternated their time in the bathroom with their time taking a turn with Bella. While it was Molly's turn to hold Bella, she scrolled through her messages and found one from Joe, Moss's oldest brother.

It's a yes on the James sporting goods project. Jess has some ideas, she'll shoot you a message when she has them together.

Molly emailed Calvin James to let him know, and received a reply almost immediately.

Why are you working so early? Do you ever sleep? he emailed.

Samperi Builders are always on the job, she emailed back.

Are they on the job during lunch today, or would you be available to meet? he asked.

Molly looked at the baby in her left arm. *I'm still on babysitting duty.*

You are a dedicated employee of both your jobs. But it seems like I won't get to hear another rejection by you in person if I don't accommodate. Bring the baby—we'll go somewhere kid friendly?

Molly bit her finger, thinking. Moss was her roommate and boss. Going out with another man for a casual lunch date wasn't cheating on him, it *wasn't. Okay,* she typed and hit send before she could change her mind.

"Moss, do you mind if I take Bella out somewhere for lunch today?" Molly asked when they were in the car on the way to work.

"No, why would I care?" he asked. "It must get lonely and boring being in the office all day every day."

"No, I like my routines. And I'm not always alone. Benny's there a lot, and Joe and Jessamine come and go."

"That's a lot of Samperi time, Mol. Maybe you should consider cultivating some outside interests," Moss joked.

"You're forgetting my once-a-week luncheons with Lou," Molly reminded him.

"Lou is almost a Samperi, both by marriage and by level of outspoken insanity," he said. "Do you have any friends outside our family?"

"No," Molly said, feeling more than a little pathetic. For years she had kept so busy trying to survive that she hadn't had time or energy for friendship. And she hadn't wanted anyone to know the truth about her, that she was homeless and living in a rotation of shelters.

"You can be friends with my friends," Moss offered. "What?" he added when Molly wrinkled her nose.

"Nothing," she said.

"No, it's something. Say it, you don't like my friends," he said.

"What's to like?" she asked.

"They've been my friends forever," he said.

"Why?" she asked. "I mean that genuinely, I'm not trying to bash you or them. What qualities make them good friends? More than longevity."

"They're funny, and we all like music," he said.

"Does your family like your friends?" she asked.

"You know they don't," he said. He was the only one of his siblings who hadn't been allowed to have his friends over. He used to think it was because his mother was more protective of him, but now Molly made him wonder. Was it because his parents had considered his friends bad influences?

"Hey, you know them better than I do. Maybe you see all their good points. All I've ever seen from them is drunken video game playing and partying."

There was more to his friends than partying, wasn't there? He tried to think of the things about his friends he liked, but he drew a blank. "I'm not giving up my friends," he insisted.

"No one said you had to," she replied.

"It seems like that's what you're saying," he said.

"Then you're not listening. Your friends are your business. All I said was that they're not my friends, and I don't have any desire to make them so, thank you all the same."

Moss still felt peeved, but he didn't know why. "They've been texting me," he blurted. "It's not like they've totally abandoned me or something. Everyone keeps asking where I've been. The band is thinking of getting back together and might play a gig at *Truckers* this weekend."

"So go," she said.

"You said I had to straighten out or else, and now you're telling me to go to *Truckers*," he said. "Mixed signals much?"

"You've been working hard and making gains, Moss. And you're not being held hostage. If you want to see your friends and have a night out, then have one. I'll watch Bella."

He sat up excited. "Come with me. We could put those baby earmuffs on Bella, I've seen babies wear those at rock concerts. You deserve a night out too, Mol."

"That's really sweet, Moss, but the truth is that I hate *Truckers*."

"How can you hate *Truckers*?" he asked.

"Because it's a post-high school dive bar that smells like beer and sadness," she said.

"You hate everything fun," he accused.

"Or maybe we have different ideas of fun," she said.

"How can you possibly think it's fun to stay home night after night doing nothing?" he asked.

Molly was stung. She'd had fun because she was with him. Apparently he hadn't felt the same and had instead felt trapped. "I enjoy stability and routine," she said quietly. "When I was a kid, that was all I wanted out of life. Now that I have it, I guard it kind of jealously." She turned to stare out the window. Moss was driving, of course. Somehow he had assumed complete control of her car.

"Are you doing that girl thing where you say it's okay if I go out but you're secretly mad about it?" he asked.

"You must have known some awesome women in your life to think that. If I say it's okay, then it's okay. If I didn't want you to go, I would tell you," she said.

"Sorry, it's just that you seem upset."

"I'm fine," she assured him.

"I may not be a smart man, but I do know what fine means," he said in his best Forest Gump imitation. "Fine never means fine."

"Sometimes fine means I don't want to talk about it right now, but it does not mean that I'm upset about *Truckers*. Go, have fun, play well, or whatever people say to someone in a band."

"That'll work," he said, and his mood was buoyant now. Molly hadn't realized how much all the changes in his life had been affecting him. Moss was an extrovert, and she had expected him to turn into an introvert because she was one. Of course he didn't want her life. He'd made that abundantly clear over the last three years.

"Mol," he said, touching her hand. "We've been here for like almost a minute and you haven't made a move to get out of the car yet."

Molly snapped to attention and looked around. They were in the parking lot of the office. "Sorry, I zoned."

"Were you dreaming about me and was I wearing clothes?" Moss asked.

"No and no," she said.

He frowned. "Wait, that doesn't make sense. What?"

She unbuckled the baby and picked up her bag. "See you later."

Moss got out of the car and bent to kiss the tip of Bella's nose. "Have a good day, baby." He straightened and kissed the tip of Molly's nose. "Have a good day, baby."

"Have a good day, Roomie," Molly replied.

"Roomie?" Moss repeated. He shook his head. "Work on those flirting skills today."

"I plan to," she told him. They waved to each other and went their separate ways.

CHAPTER 15

Molly was nervous, and she couldn't shake the feeling that she was doing something wrong. No one had been in the office when she left for lunch. She got an hour every day, but almost never left her desk. Usually that was because eating out was an expensive use of calories, and because she liked being at her office. It was a safe space for her, a genuine representation of how far she'd come. Maybe some people wouldn't think of a secretary as a success story, but those people hadn't seen where she started out. She was paid well, had full health benefits, and was valued for her work. There was absolutely nothing more Molly wanted out of a career.

Sometimes she spent her lunch hour scrolling through houses for sale. Molly's greatest dream in life was to own a house of her own, something no one could take away from her. She could do it now, but she wanted to have a substantial enough amount in savings so she wouldn't feel insecure. She had no one to fall back on, so it was vital she be prepared for anything.

But today she didn't scroll houses; today she had a date. Or was it a date? Maybe she was reading too much into it. Maybe Calvin James simply wanted to talk business. Everyone in town was curious over the rumor about the upcoming television show. Maybe he wanted to pump her for information about that. She wouldn't get her hopes up, just in case.

She felt anxious and jumpy until lunchtime, and then a terrible sense of dread. She shouldn't go; she was making a huge mistake. She was taking a newborn on a date, what was she thinking?

But she went, nonetheless. Calvin was already waiting for her at the restaurant, his radiant smile warming her from the inside and easing her doubts. Regardless of whether it was a love match, he was a nice guy, and she liked him.

"Hey, thanks for getting the afternoon off your dog walking business to meet with me," he said. He took Bella's carrier and placed it in the upside down high chair he'd already had placed at the table.

"It was no problem. I do have to rotate someone's tires and lay some carpet at two, though," she said, tapping the wrist on which she would have worn a watch, if she actually wore a watch.

"What babysitting secretary doesn't?" he asked. "By the way, I threatened to fire my secretary if she doesn't step up her game and take on a few more jobs. She said to tell you thanks."

"It sounds like she and I are going to be great friends," Molly said. She picked up her menu and quickly decided on a sandwich when Bella began to fuss. She set the menu aside and removed the baby from her carrier. "I really am sorry about this."

"I have to ask why this baby is always with you, not that I'm complaining because she's adorable. But I'm nosy. Is she your niece? Goddaughter?"

"No, nothing like that. My, er, friend is in a sticky custody situation, I guess you could say. It's complex, and I'm trying to help out for a few weeks. Apparently finding a reliable babysitter is like finding a black pearl." Though, to be fair, she had no idea if Moss was still looking for a sitter or if he had become complacent with the arrangement. And every day the thought of shipping Bella off to a stranger hurt a little bit more.

"I know a couple of people who might be willing to help, some sweet old ladies who genuinely love kids. I could give you their names, if it would help," he offered.

"That would be great," Molly said, but she wasn't sure she meant it. The thought of handing Bella to a stranger, even a sweet old lady, hurt the deepest places of her heart.

Their food arrived, and Bella began to fuss in earnest. "Here, let me," Calvin insisted, reaching for Bella. "I've been an uncle for a long time, and I'm a total pro."

"That's so sweet, but you don't have to," Molly said.

"Eat, I don't mind," Calvin said and, a few seconds after taking Bella, she quieted down and fell asleep.

"Maybe I could hire you as a sitter," Molly said.

"Actually, I do run an illegal daycare on the side, but I can't possibly take anymore kids. And I should probably find the ones I'm already supposed to be watching," he said.

"Bummer. Well, if you have an opening, let me know."

"Oh, we get openings all the time, thanks to the lousy government that keeps trying to shut us down. It's almost like they think you can't run a successful daycare from an abandoned slaughterhouse."

"The government has to ruin everything," Molly agreed.

He smiled the smile, the sweet and charming one that temporarily made Molly forget everything but him. "So, what are you going to do with all your babysitting money? Are you saving up for a bike?" he asked.

"I'm saving up for a house," Molly informed him.

'That's way better than a bike. But you work for the Samperis. Can't you ask them to build you a house? I'd do that for my secretary, if I knew how to hold a hammer or use a saw," he said.

"I should have asked for that in my incentive package. Hindsight is always better," she said.

"You were robbed, for sure," he said.

"What about you?" she asked.

"I've never been robbed by the Samperis," he said.

"Do you own a house?" she asked.

"I do, though, if you're used to seeing the Samperis' work, you should probably never see my house. It's the world's blandest and most boring ranch with zero character or decoration. Last year I hung a movie poster and felt like some kind of decorating guru. Do you have a particular house in mind?"

"Not really. I look around a lot, but I've never really seen anything that makes my heart go pitty pat," she said.

"What's your dream house? I'll keep an eye out for you," he said.

"Have you ever seen the Samperi's barn, their original house?" she said.

"No, but having gone to school with Moss, I could have guessed he was raised in a barn," Calvin said.

"It's this amazing wood and stone structure with all these beams running through the inside and a giant stone hearth in the kitchen. The way they talk about it, how everybody would gather in the kitchen, something like that is my dream," she said.

"The actual house or the Samperi family?" he asked.

Molly blushed, embarrassed that she had been so transparent. "The wood and stone and a big fireplace. The coziness," she said, hoping it wasn't a lie. "Speaking of family, Moss told me you work for your family's business."

"I was hoping to keep that a secret a while longer, in case you're a gold digger," he said.

"The secret's out, and I'm definitely a gold digger," she informed him. "You see that ten-year-old Taurus in the parking lot? That's from my sugar daddy. And, not to brag, but I also have an eight hundred square foot apartment next to a suspected meth house, also courtesy of him."

"Wow, you must be really good at extorting gifts from men who can't afford anything better," he said.

"Oh, I am. You should see my jewelry collection: cubic zirconia for miles."

He whistled. "I hope you get all that insured."

"Then I'd have to claim it on taxes, and that's an extra five bucks a year I'm just not willing to pay," she said, tapping her temple.

"You're like some kind of Playboy Bunny financial genius," he said.

"Don't call me a Playboy Bunny because I'm not there yet, and I don't want to jinx it," she said, crossing her fingers.

"We all need dreams in this life," he said.

"That's for sure. So, what's your dream, Calvin? Here, let me take her so you can eat." She set aside her fork and reached for Bella.

"Call me Cal," he insisted.

"That's a sad dream," she said.

"I aim low. Additionally, I'd like to be the first man on Mars."

"I like how you went for something realistic," she said.

"I've been training for it. Every day in my office, I spin really fast in my chair so I can get used to the changing gravitational pull and g-forces," he said.

"Does NASA know about you? Because I think they'd be really interested in your training method," she said.

"I keep emailing them, but, except for those form letters from their legal department, they never write back," he said.

"Don't give up, don't you ever give up," she said.

"Oh, I won't. Other than that, though, I can't say I have a lot of dreams. I'm a guy who gets up every day, goes to work, and enjoys spending time with my family in the off hours. Is that too pathetic to admit on a first date?"

"We're on a date? I thought this was a job interview. I knew I shouldn't have laminated my resume." She tapped her fist to her temple, and he smiled.

"We are on a date," he declared. "And it's the first time I've ever had to take turns eating with a woman while we hold someone else's baby."

"Really? I've never had a date where that didn't happen," Molly said. "I have access to an almost infinite supply of babies for just such an occasion."

"Not that I mind, truly, but maybe we could plan a date where we don't bring a baby along," he said.

Molly's heart thumped. "Maybe."

They shared a smile. Bella squirmed, giving Molly an excuse to drop her eyes. "I should get back to work."

"I should, too," Cal said. "Though it's harder to get fired when your boss is family."

"That's why I keep trying to get the Samperis to adopt me, so I can take longer lunches," she said.

"And they won't go for that?" he asked.

"They're strangely strict about who they adopt. It's weird," she said. She buckled Bella into her carrier while he paid the bill. He picked up Bella and carried her to Molly's car.

"This must be your Taurus," he said, stopping by her battered clunker.

"Only a hundred and twenty more payments, and this baby will be officially mine," she said, patting the top of the car where the paint had started to wear thin.

He whistled appreciatively. "You should give a car-buying seminar."

"I don't want everyone to know my secrets," she said.

"What about just me?" he asked, and before she could answer, he kissed her. It was a gentle kiss, first date appropriate, but Molly still felt a little off-kilter when it was over. She liked Calvin James; she liked him a whole lot. And as far as she could tell, he was practically the anti-Moss, settled, responsible, and in every way a grownup.

"Sorry," he said when the kiss was over. "Should I have asked?"

"No, I like surprises," she told him.

"Good. Keep that in mind when I show up uninvited at your apartment in the middle of the night sometime," he said.

"That wasn't you last night? I've really got to stop mixing sleeping pills with vodka," she said.

"You're just the kind of wholesome girl I've been waiting for," he said. His glance fell to her lips, as if he wanted to kiss her again, but he didn't. "I'll call you."

"Sounds good," she agreed. He opened her door for her and stood watching while she started the car and drove away.

CHAPTER 16

Everything was exactly the same when Molly returned to work, but she felt a little bit different. For so many years, she had felt a small amount of desperation, as if she were doomed to an unrequited love for Moss forever. But that was fading now. Moss was still a friend, and their lives were more interconnected than ever. With everything that had transpired—their disaster date, the arrival of Bella, the reality of having to teach Moss how to be a grownup, and meeting Calvin—her feelings had shifted more and more into the realm of friendship and out of the realm of potential love interest. For the first time in a long time, she began to see a life without Moss, away from his suffocating influence on her. And maybe there were other families out there for her besides the Samperis. Or maybe she would start a family of her own one day, and that would be enough for her. She felt excited about her future, and ready for it to begin.

"Let's do some laundry," Moss announced as he entered the office at the end of the day.

"Someone has done a complete turnaround on laundry," she said.

"That was me faking it. And the Academy Award for unrealistic laundry enthusiasm goes to…" he pretended to hold a microphone in front of Molly.

"Me, every week when I wash my clothes. And I'd like to dedicate it to every adult in the world who does the same thing," she said.

"See, why do you have to ruin it? I'm trying to make laundry fun," Moss said.

"You're right, I'm sorry. Laundry is fun. From trying to scrounge together enough quarters, to developing a hernia from carrying baskets, to the pure joy of sharing laundry facilities with what can only be described as a group of mental patients on a day pass, it's like Christmas, but every week," Molly said.

"It will be fun," Moss declared, banging his fist on her desk. "I will make it so. I refuse to spend one more evening in adult drudgery."

"Most of being an adult is about repeating drudgery, day after day after day after day," Molly said.

"Then what's the point of being a grownup?" Moss asked.

"The hope that, after forty or fifty years of daily drudgery, you can retire and take a nice vacation," she said.

He stared at her not sure if she was joking.

"And finding moments of pure joy amidst the inanity," she added. "Choosing to spend your time with people you love when you realize how valuable your time is. Earning things you've worked hard for. Contributing to society, building a family, and having the freedom to eat ice cream for supper."

"You never eat ice cream for supper," he accused.

"Sure I do," she said. "And if you ever see me eating ice cream for supper, that's your sign not to talk to me and to back away slowly."

"Why...oh, right. I guess having a sister does pay off for learning some things," he said. "Let's eat ice cream for supper tonight."

"Okay," she said.

"Really? You mean it?"

"You make me feel like your warden sometimes. If you want to eat ice cream for supper, then you can eat ice cream for supper. Being an adult means you're allowed to make your own choices. But it also means you're not free from the consequences of those choices."

"Shh," he put his finger to her lips. "Don't say consequences for the rest of the night. Say ice cream."

"Ice cream," she dutifully repeated, her lips brushing his finger.

"Now say, 'Kiss me, Moss,'" he instructed.

"Ice cream," she repeated, and he dropped his hand.

"It was worth a try." He picked up Bella and carried her to the car. They had loaded their laundry that morning, so, after driving through the ice cream place, they went straight to the Laundromat. Moss parked, and they sat in the car eating their ice cream.

"I feel like if I go inside, this is it for me; this is officially where I become an adult," he said.

"Not turning eighteen, making a baby, buying a car, or building an annex to the high school you graduated from?" she asked.

"No, just laundry," he said. He finished his ice cream and set the empty container in the console. "Tell me the plan again."

"We're going to stake out our washers and then separate the laundry."

"Why do we separate? Why not throw everything into one giant washer and be done with it?" he asked.

"Different clothes, different washing needs." She abbreviated because they had already gone over it that morning. "Why are you so nervous about this?"

"No Samperi but my mother touches the laundry. Doing it on my own is a big deal," he said. "I'm not even sure Joe knows how to do the laundry."

"You can do this," Molly assured him.

He puffed a few deep breaths like a footballer getting ready to make a tackle. "Let's do this."

Molly carried Bella, and Moss carried the massive load of laundry. "Understanding your hernia reference now," he grunted. "What have you got in here? Because you only weigh like twenty pounds, so I'm not sure how your laundry could weigh more."

"I forgot to tell you that every week I also wash my boulder collection," she said. "For the record, my last roommate never complained about it. Until he died from that heart attack while carrying the laundry."

"That would be funny if my spine weren't snapping in half right now," Moss said. He set the laundry on the counter with a heavy thump and put his hand to his back, wincing.

"For a construction worker, you're kind of a baby," she said. "And, speaking of babies, yours needs a bottle." She removed Bella from her carrier and started to feed her.

"You're going to make me sort by myself? But I'm a rookie," he complained.

"This is how you learn. Later you should learn how to vacuum and scrub the floors while I continue to sit back and supervise," she said.

"These clothes are clearly white, and these clothes are dark, but what about these clothes that are mixed?" he asked when he was done sorting.

"It depends on their material. That one white, those three dark, and that one white. Sometimes you have to make a third category, but it worked out well today," she said. "Now sort Bella's."

"I have to sort the baby's laundry, too? Why? She doesn't even wear underwear," he complained.

"But she has white things and red things. Do you want everything to be pink?"

"Everything of hers is already pink. What will it matter?" he groused but dutifully sorted Bella's laundry into two tidy piles and then poked his head into the next basket. "What do we have here?" He withdrew a pair of Molly's lacy, leopard-print underwear and held them aloft. "Which pile does this go into? Whites, colors, or naughty-naughty?"

"Stop it," Molly said, standing to reach for the panties.

"What's a virgin doing with something like this?" Moss continued, reaching into the basket and holding aloft a silk nightie.

"Moss, stop touching my underwear." She pushed Bella into his arms and scooted her basket farther away.

"I'd ask if you say that to all the guys, but we both know that you do," he said.

Cheeks flaming, Molly turned her back on him and quickly sorted her laundry.

"Come on, Mol, I'm only teasing," Moss said. "I think it's awesome that I'm the only man who's touched your underwear."

"Shut it, Moss," she said.

"Wait, are you actually angry?" he asked when she didn't turn around.

"Why would I be angry? Because you're taking something incredibly personal and turning it into a joke?"

"Molly, I'm sorry, honest. I'm only teasing you because I find it adorable-slash-amazing. Will you pretty please forgive me? Look, you're making Bella sad." He moved into her line of vision and picked up Bella's hand, using it to wipe imaginary tears.

"You're not allowed to use your baby to win arguments," she said, but she was smiling a little.

"Then what's the point of having one?" he asked. He set Bella in her carrier and dumped his laundry into a couple of washers. Molly showed him how to add soap and which settings to use.

"That's it?" he asked when all the washers had started.

"Now we wait," Molly said.

"Why does my mom always make it seem like you need a PhD to touch the washer?" he asked.

"Maybe as a way to ensure her kids will always need her," Molly said.

"Why? I think I'm going to be ecstatic not to be needed anymore."

"It's different for men, I think," Molly said.

"Yeah, my dad's always saying stuff about…" he trailed off.

Molly looked up from the magazine she'd been perusing. "Saying stuff about what?"

"About how he's ready for all the kids to be out of the house. I thought it was all talk before because it's not like they don't have the room. But maybe it's not about physical space."

Molly didn't comment. It was always better if he came to difficult conclusions on his own.

"I think my dad has wanted me to go all this time, and my mom hasn't, and they've been fighting about it," he said after a while.

"Hmm," Molly said.

"You're saying 'hmm' because everyone has known this for years, huh?" he asked.

"At least three," she answered. "Your brothers and sister have said the same thing repeatedly."

"They say a lot of stuff," he said, waving his hand dismissively. "Wait, does this mean I should listen to the other stuff they say, too?"

"Hmm," Molly said.

He put her in a headlock and kissed her cheek. "Stop making me grow. It hurts my brain."

"We had ice cream for supper and you flicked my underpants into the basket like a slingshot. I think you're safe from growing too much, too soon," she said.

"No, no more growth at all. In fact, I'm going to start regressing immediately. Give me that magazine so I can make spit wads."

Bella began to fuss. Molly retrieved her and handed her to Moss. "Here, talk to your daughter. You can list all the good parts of being a grownup for her."

"You get to drive, Bella," Moss said as he bounced the baby. "And cars are awesome. You get to date, but sometimes dating is pretty much the worst. Depends on the girl. You might go out with someone like Molly. See Molly?" Molly tried not to smile as she immersed herself in her magazine. "Isn't she beautiful? You should be like Molly, she's the best. She's nice and smart and smells amazing and, even though she tries to pretend she's Miss Innocent, you can tell by her underwear she's kind of wild. Don't be like your mom who is probably shooting up under a bridge somewhere right now." He paused, thinking. "I should probably do something about that."

Molly looked up. "You want to go look for her under bridges?"

"No, I mean like custody and stuff. Lou said I don't have any legal rights to Bella unless I go through the courts. Love Moon, uh, Tammy, could come take Bella back at any time."

Molly shuddered. "You can't let that happen, Moss."

"I know. I'll call a lawyer on Monday, but it's going to be expensive." He sighed. "I hate money and being poor. It's like being betrayed by someone I used to love."

"You can borrow money from me, if it comes down to it," Molly told him.

He blinked at her. "Molly."

"What?"

"I can't believe you said that to me," he said.

"I'm sorry," Molly said, afraid she had somehow offended him.

He gave a humorless chuckle. "Why are you sorry? I know you make half of what I do, and I know you've been saving for a house. How could you offer me your money?"

"When it comes to a choice between my house and your daughter, I would choose your daughter every time," she told him.

"You amaze me," he said, and Molly looked away, embarrassed. The washers ended, providing her with a reprieve. She jumped up to switch their clothes over, feed the machines, and start the dryers. When she sat down again, Moss was quiet. Molly didn't try to draw him out. He'd had a long night and a lot of thinking. Sometimes it was best to let information soak in slowly. She picked up the magazine and started to read while he held Bella and stared blankly into space.

CHAPTER 17

On Saturday, Molly woke early. She sneaked to the kitchen, opened her tablet, and looked up a recipe for pancakes. Since she was a little girl, she had dreamed of living in the type of family where the mother made pancakes on the weekends. She wasn't a mother, and she wasn't part of a family, but she had something like it. For as long as Bella lived under her roof, she vowed to provide the sort of care and stability she'd always lacked, even if the baby was too young for pancakes.

She mixed up the batter and let it rest while Moss slept. It was still early, and she wouldn't wake him on a Saturday. She made coffee, hoping the aroma would entice him to come out, as it so often did in television commercials.

But for Moss, the best part of waking up was apparently not coffee. He continued to sleep, even after Molly tiptoed into his room to retrieve a fussy, hungry Bella. Eventually she made the pancakes and saved his on a plate in the microwave, but still he slept on.

After noon, he stumbled out of his bedroom, groggy and rubbing his eyes. "Oh, you took Bella. I didn't hear either of you and kind of woke up in a panic."

"Sorry," Molly said. "Hey, do you want some pancakes?"

"No, thanks, I'll stick with cereal," he said. He plopped into a chair with a box of cereal and dumped it into a king-sized mixing bowl. The man had a serious addiction to sugar cereal, but Molly looked the other way. It was his cereal and his milk and his health. Later, when he wasn't looking, she slipped the pancakes into the trash. It felt like a waste, but she wasn't sure if pancakes were freezable, nor if she would ever remember to eat them after they'd been frozen.

After his breakfast, Moss took Bella and plopped in front of the television. He still wore his underwear and t-shirt but, as it was his apartment now, too, she again kept any commentary to herself. They were boxers, so it wasn't as if he were indecent, rather that it was finally sinking in that he was staying for good. She was giving up her privacy. Was she ready for that? She returned to the kitchen and began scrubbing, doing the deep cleaning she was never able to get to during the week.

"Molly, how much is cable?" he called and she could hear him fruitlessly flipping channels.

"Too much," she replied.

"We need a streaming service or *something*."

"Internet's too slow," she reminded him and smiled when he gave a longsuffering sigh. Molly wasn't into technology, but for Moss, who couldn't remember a time without high-speed internet, the struggle was real.

"Entertain me," he called.

"I'd do my famous marionette show, but I'm cleaning," she said.

"What's my thing for today, my grownup thing to learn?"

"How to entertain yourself," she said.

There was a pause, then, "That's too hard. Give me something else."

"Embrace boredom," she said.

"You're saying the same thing a different way. Don't try to trick me," he said, coming into the kitchen. He stood in the doorway and watched her clean. "I'm so bored even whatever you're doing looks fun. What are you doing?"

"Disinfecting stuff," she said. "It's a real party. You should get in on this."

"Let's do something. I need to get you out of this house," he said.

"Fine, why don't you come up with something we can do? It has to be free or cheap, and we have to be able to take Bella."

"Why don't you give me a real challenge?" he said. He snagged her laptop under his free arm and returned to the living room.

"This is hard," he called three minutes later, then, "Wait, I have something. How cheap is cheap?"

"Less than ten bucks," she said.

"Never mind," he replied glumly. "Wait, I have something."

"What is it?" she said, coming into the living room. All the yelling back and forth was beginning to remind her too much of his parents.

"It's a surprise," he said, closing her laptop with a snap. "Let me go change and we can leave."

"Change? Aren't you just going to add clothes over your underwear?"

He glanced down and back up with a smile. "Oh, honey, this is what I sleep in. I don't wear underwear."

She put her hands over her face. "I didn't need to know that. Ever."

He laughed on the way to his bedroom. "I'm joking. Or am I?"

"Don't care, never need the answer," she called after him. While he was in his room, she received a text from Cal.

Tonight?

Can't. Rain check? she replied.

If I say tomorrow, will I come off looking desperate? he asked.

Yes, she replied. *Tomorrow's good.*

"Ready," Moss said, and Molly jumped.

"Now I have to change," she said.

"What were you doing while I was changing?" he asked.

"Using eye bleach to try and erase our last conversation from my memory," she said.

"Then you have clearly never seen me in the buff because you would need to use whatever the opposite of eye bleach is," he said.

She pressed her palm to his mouth. "Stop it. Pack Bella's bag while I get ready."

"Hurry, or I'm coming in after you," he threatened.

"My door has locks," she informed him.

"I'm handy with a screwdriver," he retorted. "By the time I'm finished, you won't even have a door."

She rolled her eyes but, once in her room, she did hurry. Knowing Moss, it would be the one thing he actually followed through on. When she emerged from her room, Moss had loaded Bella in her carrier, packed Bella's bag, and was holding the stroller he'd purchased.

"You could not possibly look more like a dad right now. I'm so proud," she said, wiping fake tears.

"I could have a beer belly and be shouting at everyone to shut up while the Wildcats are on," he said.

"Work on that," she said.

"I've tried, but I'm so incredibly fit that fat won't stick out of reverence for my abs," he said, patting his midsection. Molly, who had seen him with his shirt off a few times at a jobsite, knew all too well.

"I'm ready," she reiterated, mostly to take her mind off his abs.

"Great, let's go. Follow me to fun times." He carried everything while she grabbed her purse and a couple of bottles of water.

"Where are we going?" she asked.

"Somewhere cheap where we can take a baby," he said.

Clearly he was going to keep it a surprise, but Molly liked surprises. She stared out the window, watching the landscape pass and trying to guess where they were going. After a long drive, they pulled up a long lane, one of the horse ranchers Molly didn't know. Moss parked her clunker in front of the brick mansion. "Be right back," he said, left the car, and went to ring the doorbell.

A man answered the door and smiled when he saw Moss. They talked for a few minutes, with Moss motioning a couple of times toward the car. After a while, Moss came back and opened the back door to retrieve Bella and her stroller.

"It's all set," he said.

"What's all set?" Molly asked.

"You'll see," he promised, and she did. He loaded Bella into her stroller and Molly followed them around the back of the house, gasping in surprised delight when they finally arrived. While the front of the house was plain, the back was a massive English garden with paths, sculptures—both bronze and plants—and, in the center of everything, a hedge maze.

"This is spectacular," Molly said excitedly, jumping up and down a little as she tugged Moss's sleeve.

"I thought you'd like it."

"How did you know about this place and how are we allowed to be here?" she asked.

"They're friends of my parents. We've been here a few times. I thought it was the coolest place ever, when I was a kid. I told the owner how much I loved it, and he was nice enough to let us walk around for a while."

"Moss, this might be the best surprise anyone has ever handed me," she said. "I love, love, love it. Look! A bunny." She stole up close to the giant tree shaped into a rabbit.

Molly was delighted by everything, and Moss took vicarious pleasure in her childlike enchantment. Usually she was fairly reserved, but today all reserve was gone and it was as if he was seeing behind the mask to the person she could have been if her life hadn't been so hard and made her a grownup at twelve.

"This is how to be rich," she said as they strolled through the maze. They were hopelessly lost, but neither of them cared. "If I were rich, I would have a massive garden like this, and a gardener to tend it. And I would have giant parties on the lawn, like Gatsby, except without the inevitable sad ending. And it would always be open to kids, like Michael Jackson's Neverland. And I would be like those rich ladies in magazines who are for some reason always carrying an ornate tray of lemonade. And I would say, 'Lemonade's ready, y'all, come and get it,'" she said in an exaggerated southern drawl.

"And I would wear white pants and a shirt with tiny ducks on it and shake everyone's hand, meanwhile working out billion dollar deals on the side," he said.

"Wait, why are you in my fantasy?" she asked.

"Because we're married, obviously. I thought that was a given. How else did you get rich?"

"I invested wisely," she said. "How did you get rich?"

"Our TV show became a big hit, and I was offered my own spinoff on the food channel. Then I wrote some books, mostly my memoir and a cookbook, both of which obviously became best sellers. Then I morphed into a lifestyle guru, kind of a male Giada de Laurentiis. And you were by my side the whole way, as someone who knew me when and kept my feet grounded after," he said. "I wrote the dedication of my first book to you, by the way. You're welcome."

She shook her head. "Let's say I married some old rich guy and he died, leaving me both his wealth and my independence. Hey, is the guy who owns this place single?"

"Ha, ha, ha, no. And if you keep trying to poach old men, I'm not going to take you anywhere else," he said.

"Pause here, I'm going to take your picture with Bella, for future scrapbooks," she said. She stood back and snapped a photo of him and Bella on her phone, smiling when she saw how well it turned out.

"Why aren't you in the picture?" he asked.

"Because, in ten years when she's looking at these pictures, she'll be like, 'Who's that lady?' and you'll say, 'That was our secretary.' And she'll ask, 'Why was your secretary in our pictures?' and it will open a whole can of worms."

"Or she'll point to the picture and say, 'Hey, it's Molly.'"

"Come on, Moss," she said, shaking her head.

"Come on what? Why would you not still be in our lives ten years from now?" he asked.

"Because you'll get married or I'll get married and we'll grow apart. That's the inevitable way of things," she said. It broke her heart to think of letting Bella go, but if Moss found a good woman who would love Bella as her own, it would soften the blow.

"That's not how it goes," he said, irritated.

"Tell me how I'm wrong," she said.

"You'll still be working for us, I hope. You'll still be in our lives," he said.

"As your secretary, maybe. But I'll hopefully have kids of my own by then, and maybe you'll have more kids, too. You'll bring them here with your wife, and I'll tell my kids the story of this place and how great it is. And maybe we'll reminisce at the company Christmas party about when Bella was a baby and we were roommates and how crazy it was and how tired we were."

"Molly," he said, frustrated.

"What?" Molly asked, genuinely puzzled by his anger.

"Why do you have to bring everything down and make it sad? Can't you just enjoy the moment?" he asked.

"I am enjoying the moment, a whole lot. In fact, I'm loving the moment. This day is going to rank up there with my top ten ever. Maybe my top five. But that doesn't mean I have to ignore reality," she said.

"Yes, it does. For today, suspend reality. It's you and me and Bella and always will be," he declared.

"Fine," she said, not wanting to mar the day with an argument. "It's you and me and Bella and we're going to be rich as Zeus and have a garden just like this. And, for the record, you already resemble a male Giada de Laurentiis, so you're kind of halfway there."

"Molly, Molly, Molly," he said, slipping his arm around her shoulders. "Giada wishes she looked this good."

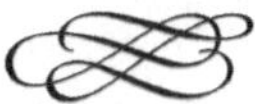

CHAPTER 18

Moss had never been more excited to go to *Truckers*. Despite what Molly said about not being his warden, he felt like he was on a day pass from prison. He didn't have to be a dad. He didn't have to be an adult. All he had to do for a whole evening was play his guitar, sing, and hang out with his friends. Before, he had taken all that for granted. No longer. Now that he knew how much work it was to take care of a baby and be an adult, he would never take precious freedom for granted again.

"You're sure you don't mind that I go," he said one last time before he left Molly and Bella at home for the night.

"Yes, I mind. Please stay home," she said deadpan, then noting his crestfallen expression, laughed. "No, now go before I actually do change my mind. And break a leg. A string? I don't know, whatever. Have fun."

"You're the best," he said, picking her up in a hug and planting a smacking kiss on her cheek before bending to kiss Bella goodbye.

"Take care of Molly, Bella. Don't eat all the Doritos."

"I don't eat Doritos," Molly assured him.

"I was still talking to Bella. She's been eyeing them lately," Moss said. Molly laughed and, with a final wave, he was on his way.

The Love Machine hiccupped a little when he started her up. "I know," he said patting the dashboard. "It's been a long time. I'm so sorry. Please forgive me." She settled into a purr, and he knew he'd been forgiven. He loved his car, loved, loved, *loved* his car. He had bought her as a scrap of junk and restored her himself, laboriously rebuilding the engine before having her painted and re-upholstered. It hadn't been cheap but, back then, he'd had nothing else to do with his money. Now his gut twisted a little at the amount of money he had poured into her. *No, no, no.* He absolutely refused to think of money or responsibility on this night of all nights.

He walked into *Truckers* expecting a little too much. A part of him hoped everyone would turn around and yell his name, announcing his triumphant return. Instead the smell of smoke rose up to greet him and stung his eyes. Their town was one of the only ones in the state that still allowed smoking in bars. Where tobacco was still grown, tobacco laws tended to be more lenient.

"How y'all doin'?" the iconic and ancient waitress, Darla, spoke. To be fair, she said the same thing to everyone and probably had for the past fifty years, her scratchy nicotine-damaged voice sounding as if it were being dragged over broken glass. Moss nodded at her and she resumed wiping down bar glasses of dubious cleanliness. Besides smoke, the bar smelled like stale beer and old vomit. Molly's words about it smelling like beer and sadness rose up to greet him. He had never thought of it that way before, but as he scanned the smoky, dimly-lit interior, he felt the weight of her words. No one looked very happy to be there. He saw his friends sitting in the corner and made his way over to them.

"Moss," a few of them yelled at his approach, and Moss's spirits felt a little bit lighter. The strangers at the bar hadn't missed him, but his friends had.

"What's up, man?" Dave asked, flicking ash into a tray on the table. Most of his friends smoked. Moss tried it once when he was twelve. It left him nauseated, and his mother had spanked him, his last ever spanking. It hadn't been the spanking that got to him—by that time they were about the same size. But her words when it was finished,

"My father died from lung cancer, Mossimo, *how could you?*" She had looked so sad and so disappointed that he had never picked up a cigarette again.

"You wouldn't believe it if I told you, man," Moss said. He hadn't yet told his friends about Bella or about being kicked out of his house. He opened his mouth to do so now when the conversation shifted to another topic. He listened and laughed until the conversation returned to him.

"Hey, Moss hasn't been here in like forever," a girl named Jayma said, lifting her empty glass in his direction. "Next round should be on him." Everyone chimed in their agreement.

"Sorry, guys, I'm broke," he said, and it was as if he had dropped a bomb on the table. He had never said those words to anyone before, and they left a bitter taste in his mouth. He wanted to be the generous guy who bought endless rounds for the table, but if he did, it meant literally taking food out of Bella's mouth and rent out of Molly's pocket.

"What's up, man?" Dave repeated.

"I had a kid," Moss confessed, and the shock around the table deepened.

"No way, aw, man, I'm sorry," Dave said.

"That's the worst," Ed agreed.

"Whose is it?" Jayma asked.

"Love Moon, uh, Tammy," Moss said and, to his chagrin, he couldn't conjure her last name.

"No way," Dave exclaimed. "I thought she was a total meth head."

"Apparently so," Moss said. "Or heroin, or maybe both."

"You better be careful, Moss. That girl is crazy," Jayma said.

"I haven't seen her since I took the baby," Moss said. "Or a long time before. I didn't even know she was pregnant."

"I knew she was pregnant; I didn't know it was yours," Jeremy said, his sheepish tone telling Moss that his encounter with Tammy had probably been more than casual.

"Can't you get rid of the baby, like give her up for adoption or something?" Ed suggested. Moss's heart knifed at the thought of letting Bella go.

"Nah, she's too cute."

"Aw, that's so sweet," Jayma said, looking at Moss with renewed interest.

"So, are we going to play tonight or what?" Dave asked. For once, Moss was glad to have the conversation move away from him. It was all well and good to be the center of attention when he was being funny, but another matter entirely to have his mistakes on display for everyone to gossip over.

"Definitely," Moss agreed. He grabbed his guitar and Jayma reached for his hand.

"Hey, Moss, do you need a place to stay? Because you could totally stay with me."

He had never particularly liked Jayma, and he had to fight a grimace at the suggestion. "Thanks, but I'm staying with Molly."

"Who's Molly?" she asked, irritated, as if Molly's presence in his life was a personal affront to her, a near stranger.

"My secretary. You've seen her before, long brown hair."

"She's hot," Dave chimed in, slapping Moss on the back.

"It's not like that," Moss said, though he had no idea why he felt the need to defend his relationship with Molly to them, especially when Dave smirked and continued to talk.

"You're saying she's available? Because I've kind of had a thing for her. All that wholesomeness needs a gentle guide into depravity."

"Ha, no, sorry, she can't stand you," Moss said and didn't feel even a little bit sorry to impart the information.

"Even better, I like a challenge," Dave said.

"Ha, yeah, no," Moss said.

Dave laughed and held up his hands in surrender. "All right, man, don't get upset. I see how it is."

Moss decided to let him continue to think whatever he was thinking. It was better than having him attempt to pursue Molly, though it might prove amusing to see Molly's reaction to Dave. He could picture the exact wrinkle of her nose when she turned him down flat, but she would do it nicely so that only someone who really knew her understood how completely repulsed she felt.

What would he do when someone, not Dave, did decide to pursue Molly? He saw the way men looked at her, even if she didn't. She was too pretty and pure to remain single much longer. The fact she had lasted this long had only been due to her strange crush on him. And he had strung her along the last three years, enjoying the ego boost she gave him, never wondering what his occasional bouts of attention and flirting were doing to her heart.

I suck, he thought as he and his band took the stage. Now that he knew firsthand how incredibly sweet, sincere, kind, and innocent Molly was, he seemed like an even bigger jerk in comparison. She was a genuinely thoughtful and selfless person, and not because she had a crush on him. She did things for everyone in the office. She kept candy out for him because he ate the most candy, but she had everyone else's favorites in her drawer. And it wasn't just the candy; she had learned all their personal preferences and quirks accordingly —Giovanni's OCD insistence that everything align, Jessamine's preference for color-coded tabs, Joe's desire to handle all his paperwork early in the morning, Benny's desire to make sure a certain percentage of the company's profits went into a charitable fund, and his own chaotic work style that often had her chasing him down on job sites to sign something before a deadline. She made working for five vastly different people, whose preferred mode of communication was yelling, seem easy.

Why was he thinking about Molly on his one night of freedom? As his band played song after song, his mind kept straying to Molly, to Bella, to home. Strange how a few days at her place had become so comfortable. He had expected to mourn for his parents' house, for their large-screen TV, for the gaming system they hadn't allowed him to take, for his mother's cooking and constant care. But he hadn't missed any of those things. He had settled into his new life like any normal person, and that could only be because of Molly, because she made him feel comfortable, at home, and cared for. He wasn't lonely when she was there; he didn't miss the opulent luxury of his parents' house when he was with her. Why? Because he had known her a long time? Because she was already a bigger part of his life than he'd realized? Because he was in love with her?

The last thought lodged in his throat and cut off his air. He croaked and stopped singing, mid-song.

"Need a minute," he said, holding up a finger.

"We'll be back in five," Dave announced, shooting Moss a curious glance. Moss didn't care, and he didn't linger to discuss anything. He darted outside, rounded the corner of the alley, and puked in the street.

CHAPTER 19

He was not in love with Molly. He wasn't. Moss leaned against the brick wall of the tavern, his head touching his knees. *No, no, no, no, no, no, no.* He was attracted to Molly, obviously. She was an attractive woman, more cute than pretty but with such alluring big eyes it pushed her over the edge into "beautiful" territory. And of course he liked her; they were friends. He had always liked her, even when he actively ran from her feelings for him. She was impossible not to like—kind, funny, and thoughtful, how could anyone help liking her? She had stepped up the kindness, taking in him and his child when they had no one else, thereby ensuring his gratitude forever. That was all this was, a combination of gratitude, attraction, and friendship. And love.

No, no, no, no, no, no. Moss had never been in love with anyone. Love was for old people, people who were ready to settle down and be responsible. Boring people like Joe, Benny, and Giovanni. Moss was young and fun, a player who was never with one woman for longer than it took to finish a sandwich. He was too much of a catch to commit himself to one person forever. It was unthinkable. And yet it was unthinkable that he shouldn't end up with Molly. How could he stomach the thought of her with someone else? How could he picture himself with anyone but her? He couldn't, and that was the problem. Ready or not, love had come for Mossimo Samperi.

He stood outside for a long time trying to catch his breath. No one came to check on him, a fact that would have escaped his notice a few weeks ago. Now it bothered him. He could be sick or dead, did no one care? He went back in the bar and grabbed his guitar. His friends were once again sitting in their corner.

"What's up?" Dave asked. His eyes looked a little glazed, as if he had used Moss's absence as an excuse to slip into the bathroom and smoke a joint. Moss was also the only one of his group who didn't do pot. Not only would his mother have been disappointed in him, but he would have lost the respect of his father and brothers. Despite anything he said to the contrary, their approval meant everything to him, especially his dad. He might be a screw-up in a lot of ways, but he always showed up to work on time, did a good job, and kept his nose clean. Until now, those had been the things that mattered most to his dad. Now his father had apparently added being a good father to his unplanned child into the mix, and Moss was trying hard to live up to that standard, too.

"Sick," Moss said, pressing his hand to his stomach. It didn't matter if he went home at this point. No one could play or sing high anyway. They would continue to sit around, laughing over whatever inane thing caught their attention until the bar closed at three. Moss checked his watch. It was barely eleven.

No one said goodbye to him when he left, and he didn't much care. The night had been a total bust. Nothing felt the same and, in fact, it had felt like an ending, as if he had been reading the last, sad chapter of a book he hadn't much enjoyed. He drove around for a while, eventually skimming through a fast food joint for a soda to erase the taste of sick from his mouth.

Eventually, when he could think of nowhere else, he went home. The fact that he had nowhere else seemed like an omen. There was only Molly, at the end of the road, and now Bella.

He let himself in and saw them sitting on the couch, Bella snuggled up and sleeping on Molly's chest. Molly was wearing tiny shorts and a t-shirt, obviously pajamas. Her long legs stretched onto the coffee table in front of her, seemingly going on forever. Moss felt like he might throw up once more. He couldn't do this; he wasn't ready. Of all the grownup stuff he'd had to face, falling in love was by far the most terrifying because it meant he'd have to be vulnerable.

"Hey, you're home early," Molly said.

"Be right back," Moss said, and shot into the bathroom. He didn't get sick. Instead he splashed his face with cold water and brushed his teeth a couple of times to take the bad taste away. When he could put it off no longer, he opened the door and stepped back into the living room.

"Did she give you any trouble?" he asked, aiming for a casual tone.

"No, she was a sweetheart," Molly said, kissing Bella on the top of her head. "I like to hold her when she sleeps, so she always knows how loved she is."

Moss bit his cheek because, for some inexplicable reason, he felt the urge to cry. *Dude, get a grip,* he commanded himself. "Do you want me to take her?"

"I'm afraid she'll wake up. I'll put her down and hope for the best." She slipped inside his room. He resisted the urge to follow by counting to one hundred in his head. She returned and partially closed his bedroom door. "Success."

"Great," he said, smiling weakly.

She tipped her head, studying his face. "What's wrong?"

"Nothing, I felt a little sick. I think it was all the cigarette smoke. Maybe I'm becoming allergic."

She eased closer and sniffed delicately at him. "Yeah, you have the *Trucker's* stench. We might have to burn those clothes."

He grabbed her and kissed her, with zero buildup and zero finesse. All he knew was that he needed her, needed every part of her, and kissing her was the only way he could think to make it happen. She responded, either by surprise or desire, he didn't care. He should have stopped it right there, should have told her what he was feeling and had a rational discussion like the grownup he was trying to be. Instead he got greedy. Forgetting himself, forgetting the baby in the next room, forgetting her innocence, his hands slipped lower on her body and he began herding her toward the couch.

She gave him a hard shove and he stumbled back a step. "Stop it."

"There's no reason to be afraid," he said, remembering how he had felt when he was still a virgin.

"I'm not afraid for me, I'm afraid for you," she said.

"I'm definitely not afraid," he told her, grinning. In retrospect, the grin was another mistake.

She scowled. "You can't do this."

"Do what?" he asked, beginning to realize they weren't on the same page.

"Moss, my mom paraded an endless supply of strange men through my life. A man was the reason we ended up in Portland. Another man was the reason we ended up on the street. Some of them were..." she looked away and shuddered. "Terrifying. Kids need stability, Bella needs stability. You have to be the dad, you have to be the stability. That means not dragging an endless supply of crazy, random women through your daughter's life because you're lonely or hormonal or whatever."

"You're not crazy or random," he pointed out.

"I'm also not a one night stand. I'm not even a weekend."

"What are you?" he asked.

"I'm forever."

He took a breath to tell her he was too, now, but she continued.

"And I'm seeing someone."

"What?" he exclaimed. "Who? How? When?"

"Calvin James. We've only had one date, but we're planning another one for tomorrow, if you'll watch Bella."

"What if I say no?" he said.

"Then I'd say you're petty and immature and I'd take her with me," she said.

He slumped. "Of course I'll keep her while you go out." He wanted to tell her, to confess his newfound feelings, but he didn't know how. He had never told a woman he loved her before.

"Thanks," she said. She pointed toward the couch. "Don't try that again. Goodnight."

"Night," he said. He sat on the couch, turned on the TV, and watched without watching for another two hours before Bella began to fuss and it was time to feed her a bottle.

The next morning, things felt tense, but maybe it was just Moss. He hadn't slept well, and he had woken up irritable.

"Why are you going out with Calvin James? Could there be a more boring person on the planet? I submit there could not."

"He's nice, and settled, and responsible, and funny," Molly informed him as she read the morning news on her phone.

"Zzzzz," he replied, pretending to sleep.

"You don't have to like him; you're not the one going out with him," she said.

"How can you leave Bella?" he tried.

"The same way you did last night," she replied, unconcerned. She was used to Moss and his bouts of jealous self-centeredness.

He liked to be the center of every woman's universe, true. But what she didn't realize was that this time was different. "I think you can do better."

She set down her phone and patted his cheek, smiling "Thanks for the vote of confidence. By the way, your friend Dave texted and asked me out. After I stopped gagging, I politely refused. What was that about?"

"I don't know," he said, glum. The whole world was against him, it seemed. "Why are you meeting him there? A gentleman picks a woman up."

"Hmm, how would that work? Come in, Cal. You remember my boss and his child, yeah, we all live together. It's just like *Three's Company*."

"*Three's Company*? I don't even know what that is, Grandma," he said.

"Hmm. I have to go."

He grasped her hand. "Don't go."

"You'll be fine," Molly assured him. "Bella's really getting into a good routine, and I wrote down her schedule, in case you had questions."

"Can I call you if she's fussy?" he asked.

"What do you think?" she said.

"Yes?"

"Sure, but if it goes straight to voicemail, it's probably because I'm out of range. For the next four hours."

"Don't have fun. And keep all of your clothes on," he said.

"Wait, you're giving love advice? I should be writing this down," she said.

"I'm trying to prevent you from repeating my mistakes. This is a very real consequence of bad behavior," Moss said, holding Bella aloft.

"Maybe spending time with her has given me baby fever," she said.

"Molly, stop it," he commanded. "Do not do anything I would do, I mean it."

"That only rules out everything I already wouldn't do," she told him and, with a final muss of his curls, she grabbed her purse and headed out the door.

Moss sat stewing in misery for a while until he couldn't take it anymore. He had given Molly the Love Machine in case he needed to take Bella somewhere, and right now he needed to take Bella somewhere. Desperate times called for desperate measures, and he had never been more desperate. Steeling his resolve, he picked up the keys, loaded up the baby, and went to see his sister.

CHAPTER 20

"I'm glad you're here," Jessamine said when she opened the door and saw Moss standing on the other side, Bella's carrier in his arms.

"Why?" Moss asked, suspicious. His sister had never been glad to see him. She was wearing jeans and a flannel shirt, something else that set off alarms. Jessamine was always overdressed for the occasion, no matter the occasion.

"I need some help cutting a pipe in my bathroom. It's stuck and I need brute strength," she said.

"What's wrong with your bathroom?" he asked.

"I didn't like the tile," she answered as she led him down the hall.

Moss set the baby's carrier on the floor and surveyed the small room. "You took it down to the studs?"

"I *really* didn't like the tile," Jessamine said. She was notorious for renovating and then re-renovating her space. Moss had sort of lost track, but he thought this was the third time she had done this particular room. At work, she was their design person. But the truth was that she was as good at remodeling as any of them, and probably a better carpenter than Moss. She enjoyed the grunt work, but design kept her too busy. So she dabbled at her own house, whenever she had time.

Moss spied the pipe cutter sticking out and crouched to finish cutting the stubborn pipe. It must be really hanging on if Jessamine couldn't do it because there were few things she couldn't do on her own. Moss suspected that was why she was still single; guys found her intimidating. As his mother liked to say about her, she could bring home the bacon and fry it up in a pan. And then build a nice cabinet in which to store the pan.

He cut the pipe, handed her the tool, and took Bella out of her carrier.

"What are you doing here?" Jessamine asked him. She eased around him and began measuring. "I'm making a new vanity," she added at his curious inspection of her work. "I need to re-rout the plumbing to come out of the wall instead of the floor."

"Of course you do," Moss said. His sister thrived on making things as complicated as possible. Remove all the support beams from a house and cantilever it so it somehow remained standing? Absolutely. "I wanted some advice."

She put down the measuring tape and began to pay attention. "In twenty five years, you have never once asked me for advice."

"I needed a woman's point of view," he said.

She sat. "Okay, go on. Here." She took the baby from him and began to absently pat her bottom. How did all women seem to know how to do that? It had taken him days to figure out how to hold the baby just right to ease her fussing, but Molly and Jessamine seemed to know how to do it by instinct.

"It's about Molly," Moss said. "She's seeing someone else."

"Okay," Jessamine prompted.

"That's it? My love life is a train wreck and all you have to say is 'okay'?"

"I guess I'm confused. Molly's made no secret of her interest in you for three years and now, when she begins to date someone else, you're coincidentally interested in her. This sounds more like a high school drama than a serious concern," she said.

"You don't understand," he said, frustrated.

"Then explain it to me."

"I held off on Molly because I knew she would require more of me than I was willing to give. But now, when I'm there, suddenly she's not," he said.

"Okay," Jess said, processing. "What have you done for her?"

"I changed my whole life for her," he exclaimed.

"You mean you finally grew up and started taking responsibility for the messes you created?" she said.

"It doesn't sound as good when you say it," he said.

"That's because it's not. Look, I'm going to say something to you that I have probably never said before: I'm really proud of you. You have stepped up, you seem to be pulling your life together and taking care of your daughter, probably even better than any of us expected. And if Molly had a hand in that, then we owe her a debt of gratitude. But growing up and loving someone are two different things," she said.

"How?" he asked. "Because people always tell me things like they assume I already know what they mean, and I'm here to tell you I don't. I have no idea what you're talking about, so if you could break it down for me, that would be great."

"Becoming mature requires sacrifice on your part, but the payoff is that you get to have good credit and a healthy body and a positive relationship with your daughter and family. Are you with me so far?"

"Yes," he said.

"Loving someone requires sacrifice on your part, and you might never get to see the payout. You give because you want that person to be happy and healthy. It's the way you're giving up sleep for Bella so she'll be well-fed and secure, do you get what I'm saying?"

"Yes, but what would I give to Molly that would make her happy and healthy?" he asked.

"That's the million dollar question. What does she want? What's her passion? What makes her thrive?" Jessamine asked. "And there can't be anything in it for you."

"She likes working and saving money," Moss said.

"Why does she like those things?" Jessamine asked.

"I don't know," Moss shrugged.

"Dig a little deeper. Where did she come from? What's been missing in her life? What makes her smile? She's worked for us for three years, Moss. Even I can answer those questions about her," Jessamine said.

"Could you tell me the answers?" he asked.

She rolled her eyes. "This isn't an eighth grade geology quiz that I'm going to let you cheat off of. Do the work, if you want the payout."

"You said there wouldn't be a payout," he said, confused.

"There might be a payout. She might learn to love you in return. But she might not. I guess you have to decide if she's worth the risk," Jessamine said.

"If you know so much about this stuff, why aren't you married?" he asked.

"Some do; others teach," she said. "I've never found anyone worth giving up my independence for. But, Moss, Calvin James is a really good guy. Tread carefully."

"How do you know that's who she's out with? I never told you," he said.

"Because I have eyes and a brain and I use them. She blushed all through our client meeting about his project," Jessamine said.

Moss groaned. "I forgot we're going to be working for him. I can't catch a break. What does she see in him anyway? I went to school with the guy for thirteen years and I have no idea what his face actually looks like. He's so mediocre."

"Can't you understand why he's exactly the type of guy who would appeal to Molly?" she asked.

"No," Moss stubbornly insisted.

"Then I guess you have your work cut out for you, but don't do the stupid thing where you make fun of his name and point out how boring he is," she said.

"That's pretty much all I know how to do," he said.

"Then learn to do better. Give her reasons to love you instead of him," she said.

"Why can't anything ever be easy?" he wailed.

"Everything for you has always been easy, too easy. You've never even had to apply for a job; you were born into a family that trained you how to work and pays you well to do it. You're healthy, you're—relatively—intelligent. You're nice looking, you have a family who loves you, and you have a friend like Molly who's willing to take your sorry self in and litter train you. I really have zero patience for your whining, today or ever. If you want Molly and you believe she's worth it, then do the hard work to get her back. Otherwise, stop complaining, be a man, and stuff your feelings deep inside and never speak of them again."

"Knew I should have gone to Benny," he muttered.

Jessamine smiled. "Be a good little brother, scurry into the crawlspace for me, and disconnect my plumbing," she said.

Bella started to fuss. "Aw, I'd love to, but fatherhood calls." A secret of many contractors was that, though they had no problem scurrying up high beams without a harness, tight, dark, spider-ridden crawlspaces often sent them running in terror. Moss was no exception, and neither was Jessamine, though she would rather die than admit a fear or weakness. Joe was too big to fit into most crawlspaces, so it often came down to a game of rock-paper-scissors between Moss, Giovanni, and Jessamine to see who would have to go in.

"Knew I should have had a baby to get out of stuff," she muttered and handed Bella over to him.

He drove home and let himself into the apartment, scanning the interior as if for clues. What did he know about Molly? He looked for a piece of paper to start a list and found her notebook, the one in which she had written his list of grownup things to learn. Not being afraid to intrude on anyone's personal property, especially hers, he sat and began to browse the notebook. First he read the list she had made for him. Most of it was pretty standard, but "Start a college fund for Bella" took him by surprise, and "Get a CAR" was written in bold and circled multiple times.

The next page was a sketch of a house that had a giant heart around it. The page after that was a hand-written recipe for pancakes with an asterisk attached to a scrawl that said, "Try with buttermilk."

He set aside the notebook and picked up the book she had been reading. He inspected the title. *Jane Eyre.* He'd heard of the book, of course, but had no idea what it was about. Molly told him it was one of her favorites and she read it every year. He opened it and began to read. Three paragraphs in, he gave up, pulled out his phone, and texted his sister-in-law, Vivian.

What is Jane Eyre about?

If she was surprised he was asking her a book question, she didn't convey it. Instead she sent a lengthy text summary in reply.

Badly mistreated English orphan goes to boarding school, gets abused, becomes a governess for a weird family, falls in love with employer who, though difficult, loves her for who she is and provides her with a true home. One of the great gothic classics. A must read.

Thanks, he replied.

Literature wasn't his thing, but even he could see the appeal of the book for Molly. It might as well have been written for her. Badly treated orphan, starts working for a weird family, falls in love with her employer. He set the book aside and determined to read it, if only to find out what the employer did that worked so well.

He carried Bella toward the front of the room and sat down in front of Molly's small and tidy movie collection. Reaching out, he took *Enchanted* off the shelf. She had once told him it was her favorite Disney movie.

"Let's see what it's all about, Bells," he said and started to watch.

Near the end of the movie, Molly arrived home and came to sit beside him on the couch. "What are you doing?" she asked.

"I have a daughter now; it's time to see what all these Disney movies are about," he said and paused the show. "How was your date?"

"Nice," she replied.

Her happy smile was like a knife to the gut. Had he kissed her? Had they done more than that? He wanted to throw up. What was it about being in love that made him sick to his stomach?

"What?" Molly asked, slightly defensively as he continued to stare at her in silence. She was probably waiting for him to make some sarcastic or cruel remark about Calvin James. A million of them ran through his head. Somehow he refrained from letting them out.

"Nothing. I'm glad you had fun, but I'm more glad you're home safe." He faced forward and unpaused the movie.

"This is my favorite part," she said as the main male character began to sing to the main female lead.

Moss paused the movie again. "Why? Why is this part your favorite? I really enjoyed the part where the animals cleaned her house."

"He's singing to her," Molly said.

"I sing all the time," Moss replied, somewhat petulant.

"He hates singing. He's doing it for her. That's romantic. Plus I like the song." She took the remote and unpaused again, smiling slightly as the characters on the screen sang and danced.

Moss faced forward again, but his mind was on Molly. He wanted to touch her, *needed* to touch her. The scent of her was everywhere and every pore of his body was urging him on. But she had said not to touch her again, hadn't she? Or had she simply been referring to his clumsy attempts to round third base with her? What if he only touched her a little, in a nice way? The worst she could do was tell him to stop it. He rested his hand on her knee in what he hoped was a companionable gesture. It represented approximately one percent of what he wanted to do at the moment, but it was all she would allow, if she would even allow that much. He held his breath, but she didn't push him away. In fact she scooted slightly closer and smoothed her palm over Bella's head a few times before resting her head on his shoulder with a yawn. A few minutes later, she was asleep.

CHAPTER 21

oss was acting weird, and Molly was beginning to grow paranoid. She suspected that he was getting tired of being an adult and looking for a way out. She had tried to take it easy on him after whatever happened at *Truckers* on Saturday. His only goal for today, Monday, was to contact a lawyer and get the custody ball rolling. Whatever the cost, he needed to ensure that Bella was safe.

She was at her desk when the door opened and Moss's mother, Mrs. Samperi, entered. Molly greeted her with a smile.

"Joe's the only one in today," she said, though she had a feeling Mrs. Samperi already knew that. Somehow she always seemed to know where her children were and what they were up to.

"Actually, I came to talk to you," Mrs. Samperi said. "I know Moss has been staying with you."

Molly winced. Mrs. Samperi's strict, Catholic upbringing didn't allow for male/female cohabitation. "It's not like that, Mrs. Samperi. We're not seeing each other. He has his own room."

"I know, dear. Don't mistake me. We're all very thankful you've given him a place to stay. It, uh, hasn't been easy, this transition. My husband is adamant we go the full two months with no contact, but I wanted to check with you and make sure he's okay."

"He's fine," Molly assured her. "He's doing well, truly."

"Oh, all right. I wondered if you might give him this for me." She laid a fat envelope on Molly's desk and slid it forward.

Instinct warned Molly to reject it. "What is it?" she blurted.

"Just something I think he should have," Mrs. Samperi replied, her eyes darting cagily to Joe's closed office door.

Wary now, Molly picked up the envelope and peeked inside. There was at least two thousand dollars inside, probably closer to three. She set the envelope down and pushed it back. "I'm sorry, Mrs. Samperi, I can't give him that. You'll have to do it yourself."

"Why not?" Mrs. Samperi asked, somewhat sharply.

"Because he's doing fine without it, and it's not my place to enable him," Molly said.

"What do you call what you've been doing?" Mrs. Samperi said.

"Helping a friend. Besides, Moss is paying me rent." She didn't mention the childcare because the older woman seemed not to have noticed Bella sleeping contentedly behind Molly.

"I would like you to give this to him," Mrs. Samperi said more forcefully, sliding the envelope forward once more.

"No," Molly said, sliding it back.

"I think it's important for you to remember who you work for," Mrs. Samperi said.

"I work for your sons and your daughter," Molly retorted.

"I know how much money he has in the bank. He needs this," Mrs. Samperi insisted.

"He's fine," Molly argued.

"How can he be fine living on a measly few hundred dollars?" Mrs. Samperi yelled, now leaning over Molly's desk.

Molly stood and leaned forward herself so they were nose to nose. "He doesn't need the money," she said.

"He does," Mrs. Samperi shouted. "If you don't give him the money, he's going to get in trouble."

"Then let him," Molly shouted in return, smacking her palm on the desk. "Let him fail, let him fall. For once in your life, stop cushioning the fall for him. Do you understand what you've done to him, how you've crippled him? He has never paid a bill, never rinsed a dish, never touched his laundry. You've raised a twenty five year old baby, and if he doesn't change soon, he's going to be ruined forever. Do you think anyone is going to want to live with him or, worse, marry him if he continues to act like a child? He can make it on his own, but you have to let him try."

"Don't tell me how to raise my child," Mrs. Samperi yelled.

"He's not a child," Molly yelled. "He's a grown man, and a really good one, if you would let him be. He's loving and caring and loyal and kind and funny, but you have to let him go." She smacked her palm on the desk again, huffing.

"Who do you think you are?" Mrs. Samperi yelled.

"She's right, Ma." At some point unseen by the two angry women, Joe had exited his office and began observing their standoff. "You've babied him to the point of crippling him. Stop it now or, Molly's right, you're going to ruin his life."

"You sound like your father," Mrs. Samperi said.

"That's because he's right, too," Joe said. "If you don't want to let him go for yourself or dad or any of us, then do it for Moss. He needs to grow up; it's time."

Without a word, Mrs. Samperi took the envelope, turned her back on them, and reached for the door.

"Mrs. Samperi," Molly called. The older woman paused but didn't turn back. "I'm sorry, I shouldn't have yelled at you. That was disrespectful and rude."

Mrs. Samperi nodded once and let herself out.

Joe and Molly were perfectly silent for a moment until she worked up the courage to speak. "Am I fired?"

"Fired?" he repeated. "Pfft. Write yourself a check for a thousand dollars and call it a bonus. Fired," he repeated, shaking his head. Laughing, he went back into his office and closed the door.

*M*eanwhile Moss was reading *Jane Eyre* on his lunch hour. Giovanni saw, did a double take, and tripped over a beam.

"What are you doing?" he asked.

"Reading," Moss said.

Giovanni looked around for the cameras. "Is this some kind of elaborate prank?"

"What's Mr. Rochester hiding in the attic?" Moss asked.

"A killer robot he designed and built, and if anyone finds out about it, he'll get in big trouble," Giovanni said.

"Huh," Moss said, turning the book over to stare at the cover. "No wonder she likes this book so much."

"What are you doing? What is it?" Benny said. Moss and Giovanni looked up to see Jessamine dragging him to them, tugging his arm as if he were an errant toddler.

"What's up?" Giovanni asked.

"You have to see this," Jessamine said. She held up her phone for all of them to see. They gathered around and, suddenly, Molly and their mother appeared on the screen, yelling at each other.

"Play it again," Benny urged when it was over.

"I've got to send this to Vivian," Giovanni said.

"Who do you think I got it from?" Jess asked. "Joe sent it to Peaches who sent it to Lou and Vivian who sent it to me."

"Do you think we could get Molly to do this on a weekly basis, about other issues besides Moss?" Benny asked. "Because I've been accumulating a long list since I've been home."

"I think we'd have to get in line behind Joe and Peaches," Jessamine said.

"Play it again, but this time louder, and is there a way to slow it down?" Giovanni asked.

"I have to go," Moss said, but they only gave him a vague nod of recognition, so engrossed were they in replaying the argument between Molly and their mother. As for him, he wasn't sure how to feel. Was he angry? Hurt? Upset? He had no idea. All he knew was that he had an urgent need to see Molly. He practically flew to the office, ran up the steps, and flung open the door.

Molly looked up, startled. "Um," he began but didn't know how to continue.

"I," she started, but also couldn't seem to find more words. And then she burst into tears, loud, weepy, dramatic tears. Moss scrambled forward and pulled her into his embrace, soothing her gently.

"It's okay," he said, smoothing his hand down her spine.

"I yelled at your mother," she mumbled after a while.

"Everyone does," he told her and she laughed, but the laughter turned into more tears, and it was a while before she got them stopped.

"I'm so embarrassed. I've never talked to anyone like that before," she said.

"No one has ever stood up for me like that before, and especially not to my mom. Outside of my Nonna, she's the scariest woman I know." Molly nodded her agreement, and he chuckled. "Just so you know, my siblings are probably planning to erect a statue of you outside the office. You're officially their hero."

She groaned and pressed her face farther into his chest. "How does everyone know?"

Now didn't seem to be the time to tell her about the recorded evidence that would live on in infamy. "You know how the Samperi rumor mill is."

"Faster than a greased pig," she said and finally took her face out of his chest to look up at him. Her cheeks were streaked with mascara, but he didn't care. To him, she was beautiful. His hand caressed her face, gently, lovingly. He had never seen her cry, and he hoped to never see it again. It hurt a place deep inside of him he hadn't known existed until this moment, something primal, and his anger finally found a target: his mother had hurt Molly, had made her cry. His mother would need to apologize and make amends. Or else.

"I think I just achieved a new grownup thing today. I've never comforted another human being before," he said.

"You're really good at it," Molly said. She reached for a tissue and wiped her face. "Hey, did you find a lawyer?"

"I did. He thinks we can avoid court if we can get her to sign off on custody. He's going to send over some paperwork for me to sign, and then I have to take it to her house, as soon as I figure out where she lives."

"I have her address," Molly said. She was still in his embrace. How long could he get away with holding her? "It's her mother's address, along with her last name and phone number. I figured we would need it at some point, so I looked it up the first night."

"How do people survive without a Molly in their lives?" he asked.

"They have a Siri or an Alexa. Hey, guess what?"

"What?" he said. He was only half listening. His thumb began making slow little circles on her spine. Maybe it was like the frog with the pot of water. If he eased her in, maybe she wouldn't notice what was going on.

"Your producer called today."

"What producer?"

"The producer of the television show you're going to be on," she said.

"You're going to be on it, too," he said.

She shook her head.

"What do you mean?" he asked.

"I mean I didn't sign a release."

"Why not? You're part of this company, part of us," he said. *Part of me, I love you. Never leave my embrace, ever, ever. Let's buy a dog together.*

"Thank you for that, but I don't want to be on television. Speaking of which, are you going to let them film Bella?"

"The way you asked the question makes me think you already have an opinion," he said.

"It's your child and your decision," she said.

"Molly," he intoned.

"I think it would be a huge mistake. She's only a baby, and it could make your custody situation worse if things turn ugly. Plus, there's a lot of crazy in the world. No need to expose her so early," she said.

"Then I won't let her on camera," he said.

"Good," she said, smiling up at him with approval. A man could become addicted to that look.

He wanted to kiss her. He needed to kiss her. He was going to kiss her. Molly must have sensed as much in his look because she suddenly stepped out of his embrace and reached for Bella, who was snoozing peacefully. "Moss, I have a confession to make," she said.

"Good thing for you I'm half Catholic. Proceed, my child," he said, clasping his hands as he had seen his Nonna's priest do at Thanksgiving Mass.

"Cal gave me a list of prospective babysitters. I spent some time looking into them. They're wonderful old ladies who would probably do an amazing job watching her."

"Okay," he drawled, still not seeing the problem. "I guess give me their information and I'll pick one."

"That's the part I have to confess. I might have accidentally on purpose shredded their contact information," she said.

He chuckled. "Why?"

"Because I don't want her to go. I love her, and the thought of a stranger taking care of her makes me want to take off my shoes and throw them across the room while saying all the words that were on my grandmother's no-no list," she said.

"What's the problem? I'd like nothing more than for you to keep watching Bella," he said. His fingers itched to touch her again. He sat on them, perching on the edge of her desk and rocking back and forth to give his baser urges an outlet.

"I'm not quite as productive as I used to be. I mean, I can still get my work done, but it's taking longer," she said.

"Honey, it's a family business. We might as well get some use out of that," he said.

"I thought maybe you should run it by the others first to make sure everyone's on board, especially Joe," she said.

"Oh, right. There's that thoughtfulness you're famous for," he muttered. "Okay, I'll talk it over with everyone and make sure it's kosher."

"Do you have to use the bathroom?" she asked, eyeing him suspiciously as he rocked on the edge of her desk.

"No."

"Why are you doing the potty dance?"

"I didn't work a full day. I guess I have energy to spare," he said.

"Let's go out to supper tonight, my treat," she said.

"You don't have to do that," he said.

"It's okay, I got a bonus today," she said.

"All right, Moneybags McGee, but after that will you do me a favor?" he said.

"What's that?" she asked, wary now.

"Will you pretty please tell me all the words on your grandmother's no-no list?"

"If you ever hear me say those words, you'd better be running away from me. I only say them when I've reached my limit," she said.

"Haven't you already reached your limit with me a few times?" he asked.

"Not even close," she said.

"Good, we have a ways to go." Unable to resist any longer, he picked up her hand and brought it to his lips. He took it as a good sign when she didn't pull away.

CHAPTER 22

olly was on her third date with Cal. It was the middle of the week, three days after their second date. Moss was watching Bella, and he hadn't given her any grief about it, as she had suspected he might. He had smiled and told her to have a good time, and that had been that. Knowing Moss as she did, she knew something was up. Something was brewing in the recesses of his unfathomable brain; what it was, she couldn't say. He had been chipper the last few days, helpful, eager, and encouraging. In short, he wasn't acting like himself at all.

"You seem distracted," Cal said, signaling Molly back to the present.

"I'm so sorry," she said, reeling her thoughts in. "Things are advancing rapidly on the secret project, and it's been kind of an exhausting week."

"I can take you home, if you like," he said.

"We met here, remember? But I want to be here, and I'm having fun. Please forgive me for my wandering mind." He was so very nice and grounded, easy to talk to and well behaved. He never tried to sneak in physical affection, as Moss had been doing all week. It was part of his new, strange behavior, to say all the things a perfect gentleman might, and then pick up her arm and nibble the tender inside of her elbow for as long as she would allow it. Which, to her discredit, was longer than it should have been. But the sensation had been intoxicating. He seemed to know exactly where and how to touch her to short circuit her usual hands-off policy, at least for a while until she returned to her senses and told him to stop. With Cal there had been a bit of handholding and a nice, predictable kiss goodnight. And that was how Molly preferred it—solid, safe, predictable.

She finished the date on a high note and let herself into her apartment, smiling. Moss was on the couch. He turned at her approach and he looked angry.

"Mr. Rochester did not have a killer robot in his attic," he announced.

"What are you talking about?" she asked.

"I finished *Jane Eyre*, and there was no robot," he said.

"What made you think there would be a robot?" she asked.

"Gio-stinking-vanni," he replied. "I'm going to stay up until midnight and then text him to wake him from his perfectly timed slumber."

Molly laughed as she sat down beside him, moving the book to the coffee table. "Why were you reading *Jane Eyre*?"

"You said it's your favorite," he said. He picked up her feet, placed them in his lap, peeled off her boots, and proceeded to rub her feet.

Molly was going to protest, she had good intentions, but no one had ever rubbed her feet before and the words died on her lips. Instead she sank against the couch and assumed what was probably a dreamy, blissful expression. She had once heard that the feet had more nerve endings than any other part of the body, and now she believed it. Nothing had ever felt so good, and she had once gotten a venti latte for free at the Starbucks drive-thru.

"You look so beautiful, Mol. It kind of kills me that it's for some other guy," Moss said.

Molly didn't reply, both because she didn't know what to say and because she was too relaxed for words. Instead she reached out a hand and squeezed his bicep. What the squeeze was supposed to mean, she had no idea. But at least it was some response instead of silence. The new Moss was making her feel off-kilter. But, sweet mercy, he was good at touching her. He had always bragged about being good with "the ladies." She had chalked it up to self-indulgent hyperbole, but now she wasn't so sure. If this was how it felt to be in the full blast of his charm, she could be in very serious trouble. Her weakness toward him was making her feel guilty because of Cal. She had just come home from a date with him, her third. She should not be sitting on the couch with another man letting him rub her feet. Should she?

She fell asleep before she could come to a conclusion. Moss covered her with a blanket and opened his notebook. "Likes to have her feet rubbed. A lot," he wrote. He had started keeping track of the things he knew about Molly, and he was compiling a fairly large list, as well as learning a few surprising facts.

For instance, she changed out her decorations for each holiday. This in itself wasn't surprising because his mother and Jessamine did the same thing, but their decorations were numerous and over-the-top. Halloween was coming up, and Moss almost cried the first time he saw Molly pull out her lone box marked "decorations" and remove one tiny pumpkin, a wooden acorn, three felt leaves, and a pinecone. She set them on the top of the TV stand and spent the next half hour arranging them. Meanwhile his mother had seven white pumpkins for the front porch alone. He wished to be able to take Molly to the design store Jessamine frequented and say, "Buy whatever you want, it's on me." But he couldn't because he was poorer than he had ever been. Just when he began to realize the value of money, he also realized he didn't have any of it.

She was also surprisingly strict about manners, maybe even more than his mother. She never ate on the couch, only when sitting at the table. And she never came to the table in her pajamas or with tousled hair or un-brushed teeth. And though she had never told Moss he couldn't do those things, he had started to observe her rules, as a courtesy to her. It was different than with Giovanni, who had the same rules. Giovanni observed the rules because he couldn't stand disorder or rule breaking in any form. Molly, on the other hand, was not as straitlaced as his brother. That was why her stringent obser-vance of the rules of etiquette had stymied him for so long. Eventually he figured out it was because that was what she believed families did —they ate at the table in their regular clothes. Once he understood why she did what she did, he found it adorable. She had no frame-work for family life, but she desperately tried to make them a family anyway.

The little talks she had with Bella were another thing he had discovered about her. She talked to the baby all the time, but only when she thought Moss wasn't listening. At first he hadn't been listening, so intent on his own thoughts and problems had he been. After a while, he began to tune in, and when he heard what she was saying, he had to close his eyes and pretend to sleep to mask his emotion. Mostly she reiterated to Bella how loved she was, how safe and protected, how much Moss cared for her, how much Molly adored her, how much fun she would eventually have with all of the Samperis. Without a doubt, Moss knew it was all the things Molly had longed to hear when she was a kid, and it did unimaginable things to his heart that she was making sure his daughter heard them every day.

Holidays were another thing. Molly loved them. His family was big into tradition and celebrations and Molly had asked him probably a hundred times for stories about what they did for each holiday. It was as if she were compiling a list marked "What families do" and using his family for a reference. He hadn't yet worked up the nerve to ask her what she did for holidays because he was afraid he wouldn't be able to stomach the answer. For some reason, they had never invited her to spend Thanksgiving with them, but she had no other family. What did she do? Where did she go? The thought of her spending that day or Christmas alone was enough to make him want to cry all over again.

One thing was for certain: he had been tempted to cry more in the last few weeks than he had all the other years of his life put together. It was as if Molly and Bella were tapping into an as-yet undiscovered part of him, the part that felt things other people felt, as they felt them. No wonder Benny was such a soft-hearted mess. Empathy was the absolute worst.

Molly woke with a start. "I fell asleep."

"You did," he confirmed, pushing down every jab he wanted to take about the dullness of her date that led her to fall asleep so soon after arriving home.

"What are you writing?" she asked.

"My memoirs. It's good stuff—people are definitely going to want to read about why I prefer Coke to Pepsi. There's a whole chapter about it."

"That's going to translate well when they make it into a movie," she said.

"I think so." They shared a smile and sat in comfortable silence. Moss had never liked quiet before, but he was beginning to appreciate it, especially when the alternative was a screaming baby.

"I've been thinking about Halloween," he continued after a while. "What do you usually do?"

"I usually sit on the front stoop with a bowl of candy and try to entice children to come over and take some. We don't get a lot of foot traffic in this end of town."

"I think I read about you in the paper last year, 'Suspicious Woman Lures Children.'"

"I couldn't get one of them to taste my gingerbread house," she added.

"I think Lou should host a party this year," Moss declared.

"Why Lou?"

"Because she has a party house and, believe me, I know party houses." Unknown to Molly, Moss had already arranged the party with Lou who, at first suggestion, laughed in his face.

"I'm in the late stages of planning a wedding, and you want me to throw a costume party?"

"It's for Molly," he had argued until she finally gave in.

"Fine, but you're going to ruin things between me and my neighbors. I never celebrate Halloween. Every year I'm careful to turn off all the lights and make my porch candy free. I've been egged twice. And now you're forcing

me to engage. What is it with you Samperis and your community involvement?"

"We should dress up," Moss said.

"As what?" Molly asked.

"Something epic," he said.

"That narrows it down."

"You don't seem excited," he noted.

"I am. I think it sounds fun, but Cal already asked me to spend Halloween with him."

Moss thought his head might actually pop off his body. He wanted to break things and yell all the words on Molly's grandmother's no-no list. Instead he forced a smile and said, "Bring him."

Molly regarded him warily. "Will you be nice to him?"

"Yes. Maybe I'll bring a date." What was he doing? He could almost hear a narrator in the background saying, "Moss did not want to bring a date."

"Who?" Molly asked.

"I haven't decided yet," he said, mostly because his mind was a total blank. How was it possible that he was now bringing a date to a party he was planning for her?

"Colette?" she guessed, recalling his high school girlfriend.

He grimaced. "Colette? I haven't gone out with her in years."

"And yet you stuck your tongue down her throat a few months ago at *Truckers*," she said.

"Oh, that," he said, waving his hand dismissively. "That was like a 'hey, how have you been' kiss. We went our separate ways after that. I think she went home with Jeremy."

"Huh," Molly said, inspecting her nails.

"I take it you saw that kiss, the night I invited you to *Truckers*," he said.

"Maybe," Molly said, beginning to pick at a cuticle.

He took her hand, sparing her nail bed from further assault. "Don't take it out on your hands. I admit it, Molly. I was a total jerk. But you said you believe in redemption, and I'm trying to do better."

"You're doing better," she assured him. "You're doing great."

"But you're still not sure you trust me, and you're holding your breath to see how long it's going to last," he guessed.

"I didn't say that," she said.

"It's what you're thinking. I'm learning to read that large capacity brain of yours." He had eased closer until there was no space between them. He reached out and gently brushed her bangs away from her face.

"That's not all I'm thinking," she said.

"What else are you thinking?" he asked.

"That I'm attracted to you," she confessed.

"I'm glad we're on the same page," he said. He leaned in to kiss her, and she held up her hand.

"But…"

"No but," he said, shaking his head, which had the unintended consequence of tossing his curls over his eyes. Now it was her turn to reach out and push the hair away.

"But you and I are in a complicated situation, and adding anything into that mix right now seems combustible. And I'm dating Cal. I've never dated anyone who treats me nicely and doesn't pressure me for sex. I don't want to hurt him."

"I want you to be happy and healthy," he said. "But also, I just want you."

The tension between them was unbearable as Molly seemed to waiver between her heart and her head. Moss knew he was what her heart wanted while her head told her to choose Cal. The trick, he supposed, would be to convince her head that he was also the right choice. To do that, he had to hold back, to refrain from pushing her, to let her come to him. He had never not gone after a woman he wanted before, full throttle. And he had never not scored whichever target he chose. But he had never loved anyone before, never adored anyone the way he did her, and the stakes had never been higher. Losing Molly was unthinkable, so he did the impossible and did nothing. He sat and watched while the war waged within her.

Her breathing became labored, as if he actually were kissing her. She bit her lip and slowly reached a tentative hand toward his chest.

Before it could land, Bella started to wail from his bedroom. Molly froze as if she had been caught in the act of stealing a pack of gum.

"I'll get her," she volunteered before racing out of the room.

Moss lay back against the couch and closed his eyes, his heart thumping painfully. *So close, but still so far.*

CHAPTER 23

The Halloween party would be the company's last hurrah before production began on their new television show. The home and garden channel had ordered a pilot, and if they liked how it turned out, they would order an entire season. Everyone was anxious and nervous and trying not to show it, so the party couldn't have offered a distraction at a better time.

"I can't believe I let you talk me into this," Lou said when Moss, Molly, and Bella showed up at the party. Moss was Mario, from the videogame, and Bella was Yoshi, his dinosaur sidekick. He had tried to talk Molly into being Luigi, but she knew how that would go over with Cal. Instead she had agreed to be Mary Poppins, also Moss's idea.

"It looks amazing in here," Moss said, giving Lou a side hug.

"Thank Molly, it was all her handiwork," Lou said. Molly had spent the afternoon setting up the party, at the family's insistence since everyone knew she was dying to do it anyway.

"It's easy when you have a house that looks like this and six bags of unopened Halloween decorations," Molly said. Lou's house was a massive midcentury modern ranch with an open floor plan and a pool out back. It was too cold for swimming but warm enough to have part of the party staged outside and the rest in the living room. Molly and

Moss were the first to arrive, mostly because Molly was so excited she couldn't stand to wait any longer.

"Jess bought the decorations," Lou informed her. "If it were up to me, I would have put out a pumpkin and a banner that says, 'It Is Halloween.'" She had dressed as Jean Grey, from the X-men, and her fiancé, Benny, was Professor X.

"How did you survive in this thing for so many years?" Benny asked as he wheeled up to them in Lou's old wheelchair. Or at least he tried to wheel up to them. Instead he rammed into the corner of the wall, rebounded, and almost upset the entry table.

"Better than that," Lou said. "Let me teach you how to steer. Here, you are in charge of passing out candy." She set a giant bowl of candy into Molly's arms.

Molly gasped. "You bought full-size candy bars? You are like the holy grail of trick-or-treat."

"I know, I'm going to get kids every year after this," Lou groused before pushing Benny away for a lesson in wheelchair maneuvering.

The doorbell rang. Molly ran to answer it and deposited a candy bar into each of three bags. The kids went away excited and she remained at the door, watching them go with a smile.

"Are you happy?" Moss asked.

"So happy," Molly said, turning to beam at him. She reached up to smooth down half his mustache. "You make a studly Mario."

"That's because Italians rule. Next year I'm going as Stallone."

"I could be Dolly Parton. Did you ever see that movie they were in together?" Molly asked.

"No, but I'm definitely in favor of you as Dolly Parton," he said.

"It was horrible. We should rent it sometime for laughs. She has to turn a New York Stallone into a country singer," Molly said.

"That sounds amazing, and almost like my real life," he said. They laughed, and Bella began to fuss. She was showing a real preference for Molly lately. Molly wasn't certain if it was because she spent more time with her or because it was a developmental stage. She hoped Moss didn't have hurt feelings over it, but so far he didn't seem to mind.

"Someone wants her Molly," he said and handed Bella over.

"I know, baby," Molly soothed, kissing Bella's cheeks and snuggling her close. Almost immediately, she settled down, seeming to nestle into Molly's chest. "Did you hear from the lawyer today?"

"Yes, and no luck." Tammy had moved out of her mother's house. Her mother had no idea where to find her, so Moss was having to keep a lawyer on a retainer to try and track her down to get her to sign the custody agreement. "It's looking like we're going to have to go to court."

"Yuck," Molly said. He had already had to take a genetic test to verify that he was, in fact, Bella's father. But that was just the beginning of the long, legal road. According to the court system, Tammy had all legal rights to Bella, and Moss had none. He had to petition the court for sole legal and physical custody, giving him not just the right to raise her but to also make all decisions regarding her wellbeing. Tammy's mother was fully onboard, especially after Moss told her he wanted her to remain in Bella's life. But Tammy was a question mark. No one could find her to ask if she wanted to do it the easy way or the hard way. The uncertainty left a queasy feeling in Molly's stomach. At any time, Tammy could show up and demand Bella, and, legally, they would have to hand her over. And the legal process to change that seemed to be taking forever. Moss was feeling the stress as well. And the court fees were astronomical.

"It's going to be fine," Molly assured all of them, but especially Bella. "We're going to keep her safe, and nothing is going to go wrong."

"I know," Moss agreed. "She's going to be safe; we're all going to be safe."

Molly looked up at him, blinking. Safety was her keyword. She had yearned for it through all of her adolescence and worked to establish it in all the years since. It was almost like he knew that, but how could he? Lately he seemed to be reading her thoughts. And not just reading them, but acting on them. He had put a major emphasis on safety, stability, preparation, and tradition. Those were the anchors on which

Molly was trying to build her life, and Bella's, and Moss seemed to have picked up on the theme.

"Mol, you look at me like that and…"

Molly never got to hear the end of the sentence because suddenly Cal was standing on the other side of the door. She jumped, startling Bella, and opened the door.

"Hey, pretty," he said, leaning in to kiss her. "And hey, little pretty. Long time, no see. Look at you, you're getting so big." He smoothed his hand over Bella's head, smiling. "I didn't know you were going to be on duty tonight."

"She's not," Moss said, trying hard to tamp down his irritation. Calvin might have the right to touch Molly, but Bella was still fully in his control. He reached for her, and she fussed with temper, wanting to go back to the soft shelter of Molly's reach.

"Cal, you remember Moss Samperi. Moss, Cal James."

"Sure, I remember. Hi, Moss. How's it going?" Cal said, his pleasant smile encompassing his face.

"Good. Nice to see you, Cal. Molly says good things." It was the best he could do. If he stayed, everyone would regret it. He spun and strode quickly away.

"Is he getting in on the babysitting action now, too?" Cal asked, confused by Moss's abrupt demeanor.

"No, um, Bella's his."

Cal blinked at her and she tried hard not to drop her eyes. She had never lied about Bella's parentage. But she hadn't exactly been forthright, either.

"Bella belongs to Moss?" he asked.

She nodded.

"So you've been babysitting your boss's baby all this time?" he asked.

She nodded.

"And you didn't tell me why?"

"It's a weird, complicated situation surrounded by scandalous gossip," Molly said.

"Any other secrets you'd like to divulge?" he asked, half joking.

Now was the perfect time to tell him she and Moss were roommates, but before she could say anything, more trick-or-treaters showed up.

"I thought you were going to dress up," Molly said when the kids had gone.

"I did, I'm an account executive," he said, glancing down at his shirt and tie.

"But you are an account executive," she said.

"See? It works on so many levels," he replied. More trick-or-treaters arrived, followed by Vivian and Giovanni. She was dressed as some sort of instrument, and he looked very much the same, except he was holding a bowstring.

"A cello and Yo Yo Ma," Vivian explained before they could ask.

"Kill me now, I've never been more humiliated," Giovanni said.

"Literally your only concession to this costume idea was to hold a bow," Vivian chided.

"And it's already too much. Adults should not dress up for Halloween."

"Truth," Cal said, and the two men high-fived. Vivian and Molly shared an eye roll.

"Aren't you glad the fun police showed up?" Vivian asked. "I'm going to find Lou and see if she needs anything. Come on, Yo."

"Don't call me that," Giovanni said, but he allowed her to lead him away.

"I always liked them," Cal mused as he watched them walk away. He left the rest unspoken, but Molly knew what he was thinking. He hadn't liked Moss, and the feeling had been and was still very much mutual.

Joe and Peaches were the next to arrive. Joe was dressed as Wreck it Ralph, and Peaches made a convincing Vanellope.

"Hey, Molly girl," Peaches said, giving her a big hug.

"You got him to dress up," Molly exclaimed. She hadn't thought Joe would cave.

"I have to bake him a cobbler when we get home," Peaches said.

"And..." Joe prompted.

"And do it while wearing the black wig," she said, blushing faintly.

She turned curiously to Cal.

"This is Calvin James," Molly said. Cal smiled and held out his hand to Peaches who took it and shook, still looking confused.

"Cal, how are you doing?" Joe asked, stepping forward to also shake hands. "We're looking forward to getting started on the project this week. If you have time later, we could talk about..." He caught sight of his wife's expression and cut off mid-sentence. "Or we could not talk business tonight and concentrate on having fun with our loved ones."

"You read it just like I wrote it," Peaches said, patting his arm approvingly. Molly smiled, glad to see that some of the horrible tension had eased between them for a while.

"Is her name really Peaches?" Cal asked after they'd walked away.

"No, it's..." Molly began, but more trick-or-treaters showed up, cutting off her sentence. After that a few more party attendees arrived. Molly didn't know them, so she directed them to Lou, presuming they were friends of the hostess.

After another round of kids, a lone woman arrived on the doorstep. "Lou's in the back," Molly informed her, as she opened the door.

"I'm looking for Moss," she said, and then she and Cal caught sight of each other and did a double take.

"What are you doing here?" he exclaimed.

"I'm on a date. What are you doing here?" she asked.

"I'm on a date," he said. "With her." He pointed to Molly who waved awkwardly. She still had no idea who the woman was.

"I'm Amelia," the woman said, smiling gently at Molly. "And I'm looking for Moss?"

"I'm Molly," Molly replied, somewhat hoarsely. The woman wasn't beautiful. She was rounder and softer than Moss's usual type, but she had intelligent eyes and a kind smile. "I'll take you. Can you watch the door?" She thrust the bowl of candy at Cal without waiting for an answer and began to lead Amelia toward the back of the house.

Moss was talking to one of the men Molly didn't know. Bella was across the room and, to her surprise, sitting in Benny's lap while he talked softly to her, looking love struck. "Moss," Molly said gently. He looked up at her with a smile of welcome that switched to Amelia when he caught sight of her.

"Hey, you made it. Good to see you," he said, coming forward to kiss her cheek.

"Thanks for the invite," she replied. "I haven't seen you in forever." She reached up to adjust his mustache.

"Yes, the mustache is fake, but the rest is all me," he assured her, and she laughed.

Molly spun and returned to the door. She took the bowl of candy back from Cal. "Want to sit outside?"

"Sure," he said and opened the door for her. They sat on the step, but there were no trick-or-treaters in sight.

"How do you know Amelia?" she blurted.

"High school girlfriend," he said, giving her a sheepish smile.

"Huh," Molly said, turning forward to hide her smile. She was going to kill Moss, literally kill him. Of course he would invite someone relevant to Cal's life tonight. "Were she and Moss friends?"

"Strangely, yes," Cal said, as if he couldn't understand it. "She insisted he was deeper than he seemed, and, to be fair, he was always nice to her."

"But he wasn't nice to you?" she guessed.

"I can't say he personally was a bully, but that was the kind of group he hung around with. The kids who sat at the back of the class and made jokes the whole time. He was funny, I'll give him that. But, even though we weren't mortal enemies, we also weren't friends. And I'm sure he'd say the same about me."

He has, and then some, she thought. "Why did you choose to go with them to build your store?"

"Because they're the best, and because I'm giving him the benefit of the doubt that he's grown up since high school. I know I have."

"How?" she asked. "How were you different in high school?"

"I was shorter," he said, and she laughed. "How were you different in high school?"

"I was homeless," she said without thinking. She hadn't told him anything of her past yet.

"What?" he turned to her with a smile to see if she was joking and quickly realized she wasn't.

"Surprise," she said weakly.

"What happened?" he asked.

"It was one of those things," she said, mentally kicking herself. She hated divulging personal information, and especially not to someone like Cal who had always known the loving care of a family. And a wealthy family, to boot.

"Well, I'm glad you finally found a home, Molly O'Ryan," he said, slipping his arm around her shoulders and kissing her cheek.

"Thanks," she said. "Now please change the subject to literally anything else."

"I think we should go away together," he said, and Molly choked, sputtering and coughing on an air bubble that got trapped in her windpipe. "I take it that's a yes," he continued when she held up a finger and gasped a few times for oxygen.

"Sorry," she said, her throat still scratchy and raw from coughing. "What?"

"My parents have a cabin at Lake Cumberland. And there's a boat. It would be a good time."

"Oh, that sounds nice," Molly said.

"I thought so, but when you say it, it kind of sounds like I suggested prison," he said.

"I'm sorry. I thought we were taking things slowly," she said.

"I wasn't proposing," he said, somewhat defensive.

"Are you suggesting we share a bedroom while we're there?" she asked.

"I was kind of thinking along those lines," he said.

"See, that goes back to taking it slowly. I've never...I haven't...I don't rush into physical relationships," she said. "I'm careful, I like to take things slowly. Slowly." She drew the word out to multiple syllables.

"Oh," he said. "That's fine. Believe it or not, I'm kind of slothful in that category myself." They sat staring into space a few minutes, the silence between them heavy and awkward. "Just for reference, when you say slowly, are you talking weeks, months, years, or decades?"

"I don't know. But I know I'm not there yet."

"Okay," he said.

The awkward silence returned. "If this is too much for you, you can…" she let the suggestion hang, half-hoping he would decide to end things. She liked him, she really did, but the growing tension between her and Moss was casting a pall on her relationship with Cal.

"Whoa, easy there, Trigger. I said it was fine, and I meant it. I like you, and you like me, and that's where we're at right now, right?"

"Right," she agreed.

"See? We're fine."

"Good. I'm sorry if I seem a little snappy. There's a lot going on at work right now."

"Plus you're still babysitting your boss's baby," he added.

"Moss isn't just my boss. He's my friend," she said.

"Moss is friends with a lot of women," he said.

"Don't," she snapped.

"Sorry," he said, equally as terse. They sat in painful silence a while longer until he stood. "I'm going for some water. Do you want anything?"

"No, thanks," Molly replied, trying not to feel relieved when he went away. She sat on Lou's porch a while longer, handing out candy to any passers by. It was exactly the Halloween of her dreams. When she was sure the stream of kids had come to an end, she went in search of Calvin and a truce.

CHAPTER 24

The cameras had arrived. Moss found it more stressful than he'd been expecting. Though, to be fair, every area of his life seemed stressful right now. He had no money, no usable car, a lawyer to pay, a baby to take care of, and custody to obtain. Tammy still couldn't be found, the case was moving like molasses, and every available dollar was going toward funding the lawyer. They had recently started the James Sporting Goods project, and the cameras were on them all the time, during which they were supposed to act as if the cameras weren't there.

It was harder than it looked and none of them were succeeding at it. And then they got in a royal family argument and completely forgot the cameras were there. Jessamine, as usual, decided at the last minute to change the design, throwing the timeline, budget, and project length into chaos. World War III erupted, as it did whenever she changed everything at the last minute.

When the argument was finished, Joe apologized to the cameraman and production crew who replied, "Are you kidding? That was reality TV gold." And that was that, they would soon become the yelling Samperis on television.

"Mom's going to freak if everyone sees us arguing on TV," Benny said.

"Maybe it won't sound like arguing to her. Maybe she's so used to it, it will sound like when Charlie Brown's teacher talks," Giovanni said. "A bunch of background noise."

"And Nonna?" Moss asked.

"No, Nonna's going to freak. Dibs on not going to Thanksgiving this year," Joe said.

"I'm not going to Thanksgiving anyway," Moss said.

"Right, good one," Giovanni said, chuckling lamely.

"I'm not," Moss said.

"Does Ma know this?" Joe asked.

"I don't know what Ma knows," Moss said.

"Moss, Thanksgiving is two weeks away. If you don't show up, she's going to have that aneurism she's been promising," Jessamine said.

"I've had other things on my mind," Moss said, but the truth was that he was still angry with his mother. Inevitably, word got back to her. Or maybe she actually did have him wired somehow. However she found out, she showed up at the apartment that evening, coincidentally after Molly had taken Bella to the store.

"Hello, son," she said when she had knocked on the door and he answered.

"Hi, Ma," he replied.

"Are you going to invite me in, or do you leave your mother on the doorstep?"

"Come in, Ma," he said, moving aside so she could enter. She took a couple of steps inside and looked around.

"Reminds me of Brooklyn," she said and Moss couldn't tell if it was an insult or a statement of fact. His relatives who still lived in Brooklyn lived in similarly tiny apartments.

"Have a seat at the table, Ma. I was cleaning up. Do you want something to drink?"

"Water would be nice," she said.

He retrieved a glass of water for her, set it on the table, and resumed putting the dishes away. His mother watched him in silence. Moss couldn't tell if she was radiating approval, disapproval, or neither.

"Your two months is up," she said at last.

"So it is," he agreed.

"I think it's time for you to come home," she said.

"What?" he said, looking at her in surprise.

"Your father agrees," she hastened to add. "With all that's going on with the baby and the lawyer, you can stay at home until you get that worked out."

"I'm not coming home, Ma."

"Why not?" she said.

"Because I live here now," he said.

"You mean you live with Molly now," she amended, frowning.

"It's not like that. Molly has a boyfriend." He almost choked on the word.

"Then what is going on? I don't understand any of this, Mossimo. Are you mad because your father kicked you out? You know that wasn't my idea, but sometimes you have to go along with a person because you love him."

"I'm not mad about that, Ma. It was for the best; it was time."

"Then what's with the cold shoulder?" she asked.

"You really don't know?" he asked.

"If I knew, would I be askin'?" Her accent deepened when she was angry. Right now she was so angry she sounded like a Bensonhurst taxi driver.

"Ma, you treated Molly horribly, you attacked her, you made her *cry*."

"She yelled at me, too, you know," he said.

"She apologized for that. Have you done the same?" he said.

"I have nothin' to apologize for," she said.

"You came to her place of work, tried to force her to do something against her will, treated her like the help, and then left without a word."

"What about what she did?" she yelled. "All I wanted was for her to pass something along to you, and she wouldn't. And, despite what fairy tale you want to believe, she is, in fact, the help. She's a hired employee of our family company and she disobeyed a direct request. That's insubordination."

"Do you even hear yourself right now? All Molly did was try to protect me," he said.

"From your own mother? From money you desperately need?" she said.

"My money concerns are my own problem, Ma."

"You haven't always felt that way," she said.

"I have been working since I was fourteen and paying for all my extras myself for all that time. Yes, I counted on you to pay my bills for me, but it was with my money," he said.

She twisted her lips and quirked an eyebrow at him.

"What, are you saying you've been padding my income?" he said.

"I covered the extra when you ran short, so you wouldn't get dinged on your credit," she said.

"If I had known I was running short, I wouldn't have spent so much," he said.

"You've never been a saver, Mossimo," she said.

"I never had to be, but now I do, and I am," he said. "Look around, Ma, it ain't the Taj Mahal here. But I'm doing all right."

"The lawyer," she began, but he cut her off.

"Is my concern."

"And Molly's, I presume. I know she offered to give you money for the lawyer. Apparently she won't pass along my 'enabling' money, but has no problem enabling you with her own," she said.

When that got no response, she cut to the chase. "Are you coming to Thanksgiving or not?"

"Not," he said.

"And why not, or am I not allowed to know that, either?"

"Because I can't afford a plane ticket to New York," he said.

She chuckled. "Don't be silly. Of course your father and I will pay for your plane ticket."

"And Molly?"

"What about her?"

"Is she invited to Nonna's?"

"Nonna's is for family only," she said.

"That's not how it went for Peaches before she and Joe were married," he pointed out.

"That was different. Peaches was a child, she had no one else; she needed us."

"Molly has no one else; Molly needs us, and I need her. And Bella needs her."

"Bella would be fine with me," she insisted.

"Bella doesn't know you, Ma," he said.

"Whose fault is that? You know I'm always available, but you have your secretary doing double duty as a nanny. What is it with this girl, Moss? How has she got her hooks so deep into you? She's a good secretary, but come on. She's not *that* pretty."

"Ma," Moss exclaimed, smacking his palm on the table. "Enough. Molly is the best friend I've got in the entire world, and you have no idea what you're talking about. And until you're willing to admit that and apologize, then we have nothing more to discuss."

She sat frowning at him a moment before trying one more track. "You're going to break your Nonna's heart."

"I'll call Nonna and tell her how sorry I am to miss," he said.

"She's not going to get to see the baby. This could be her last Thanksgiving."

"She already has pictures of the baby, and you've been saying it could be her last Thanksgiving for two decades."

"You sent her pictures of the baby?" she asked, surprised.

"Molly did. And she has some for you, if you want them," he said.

He could see pride and desire for the pictures waging war inside her. "Not right now," she managed to choke at last.

"Fine. Ma, will you please do me a favor?"

She softened and reached for her purse, presumably her checkbook. "What?"

"Will you watch the video, preferably with dad?"

"What video?" she asked, puzzled.

"Ask Joe. He'll know what you mean if you tell him it's from me," he said.

She blinked a few times in confusion. "All right, if I figure out that code, I'll try to get on it."

"With Dad. Promise," he said.

"With Dad," she agreed. She reached out and touched his hand. "I love you, Mossimo, always."

He covered her hand with his. "I love you too, Ma. But I'm mad, and I'm disappointed."

"That makes two of us," she said. She withdrew her hand from his and let herself out.

Moss remained at the kitchen table, staring into space, exhausted and deflated.

"What's the matter?" Molly asked when she came into the kitchen a while later, her arms loaded down with Bella's carrier and groceries. "Are you sick?"

"Yes," he said.

She set everything down and reached out a hand to his forehead. "You don't feel warm."

He gathered her close and pressed his face to her stomach. "My mother was here."

"I'm so sorry," she said, hugging him in return.

He breathed in and out a few times, gaining strength from the scent of her. "Molly."

"What?"

"Please don't ever make me go back to my parents' house," he said.

"And give up all this?" she said, laughing. He pulled his face back to look up at her, and she cupped his cheeks with her hands. "Do you want me to make cookies? I bought chocolate chips."

He nodded. He was the better chef, but she was a better baker.

"What else would make you feel better?" she asked, her soft voice oozing sympathy. It was so much better, Moss realized, to be babied by a woman than by one's mother.

"This," Moss said. "Just this." He pressed his face to her stomach again and felt a little of his stress drain away. Her fingers gently trailed over his scalp and he closed his eyes.

"If you want cookies, you have to let me go," she said.

"I want you more than cookies," he said. Predictably, Bella began to fuss. Molly stepped away to retrieve her. "The baby has a vendetta against my love life."

"Your love life is how the baby got here," she pointed out.

"Don't be rational, Molly. It's unbecoming," he said.

Smiling, she turned toward the counter and began preparing the cookies one handed, cradling Bella in her other arm and occasionally bouncing to keep her happy. Moss rested his head on the table and watched, fully believing it was like watching a little bit of heaven on earth. Why had he ever wanted more than this? He couldn't remember. All he wanted now was for it to be well and truly his, for Bella's custody case to go through, and for Molly to dump her boyfriend and be with him instead.

He was putting in the time and effort it took to care for both of them. He could only hope there might someday be a payout for all of them.

CHAPTER 25

For Thanksgiving, it was just Moss, Molly, and Bella. All the other Samperis and Lou went to Brooklyn as usual. Moss wondered if he might feel sad or left out, but he was too busy. He and Molly decided to do the day as if it were still a grand celebration, so he roasted a turkey while she handled the trimmings and baked an apple pie.

"We're going to be eating this stuff for days," Moss said, reclining away from the table with his hand on his stomach.

"We can freeze it," Molly said. "And I'll make soup from the carcass. My grandma used to do that. If we play our cards right, we won't have to buy groceries for a week."

"Good because I'm out of money," Moss said. Lawyer fees were tapping him dry and his bank account was running on fumes, except for the emergency savings account Molly had set up for him. It had a thousand dollars now, and that had never seemed like so much.

They spent a lazy afternoon napping and watching bad movies they had each picked to amuse the other. It was so much fun to watch such horrible movies that they decided to make it an annual tradition. In the early evening, they took Bella on a walk around the neighborhood and then came home for round two of food.

"This is my favorite Thanksgiving ever," Moss declared as he sat on the couch that night, a food coma rendering him useless for much else.

"Really?" Molly said. "But you're usually with your family."

"I'm still with my family," he said.

"Oh, Moss," Molly said. She linked her elbow with his and rested her head on his shoulder. All in all, it had been a perfect day, one of the best in Molly's life. Not that she and Moss hadn't argued. They bickered whenever they had to share the kitchen or when Bella wouldn't stop fussing and they began to blame each other for their combined inability to make her stop. Molly, who used to believe any argument meant the end of a friendship, was slowly learning that disagreements were part of the relationship and not something to be avoided. It was all about how to argue and how to make up, and the Samperis were masters of both.

Her phone beeped with a text from Cal.

Happy Thanksgiving, Baby!

Happy Thanksgiving, Molly replied. *How's Lake Cumberland?*

Lonely, he said, and Molly left it at that.

He had been not so subtly increasing the pressure to go away with him. Molly wasn't ready, in fact wasn't sure she would ever be ready. She liked him, but when she tried to imagine handing him her virginity, the image wouldn't form. If she were being honest, she wanted to wait until she was married. She had waited this long, and the idea appealed to her on several levels. But if Cal's reaction to her reticence was any indication, she couldn't imagine any man ever agreeing to the idea.

On the Saturday morning after Thanksgiving, Molly woke to the smell of food. She checked her clock, saw that it was before eight, and stumbled to the kitchen groggy and disoriented.

"What are you doing?" she croaked to Moss who stood with his back to her at the stove.

"Making pancakes," Moss said.

"Why?" Molly blurted. She had offered to make him pancakes on the weekend no less than five times, and he always refused.

He turned to smile at her, spatula aloft. "Because sometimes dads make pancakes too, Molly."

"Oh, Moss," she quavered, pressing her fists to her eyes to push back the tears.

"Don't go mushy on me, O'Ryan. The baby needs fed," Moss said. She nodded and turned to get Bella. "Nice jammies," Moss called.

Molly looked down to realize that she was still wearing the tiny shorts and t-shirt she had slept in. She never came to the table in her pajamas, preferring to shower and dress before she emerged. "You saw nothing," she called.

"No, but I have a stellar imagination," he replied.

When breakfast was over and the kitchen cleaned up, they sat in the living room deciding what to do for the day. It was chilly and rainy and Molly didn't particularly want to go out. But Moss was a social creature and not used to staying in so many days in a row.

"We could watch football," she tried. "The Wildcats are playing today."

"We could go out and watch them play," he countered.

"You want to take Bella to a loud, smelly sports bar? Plus, we'd have to pay."

"Why doesn't the library show sports?" Moss mused. The library had become their refuge the last few weeks, when they needed to get out of the house and go somewhere free. Moss couldn't stop mocking himself for the person he had turned into, but Molly had always embraced the wonders of a public library. "I wonder if we could break into Lou's house. She has that massive TV, sitting there alone and friendless."

"Let's brainstorm some more before we turn to a life of crime," she said.

"I bet this is how Bonny and Clyde got started," he said.

"Because they were looking for somewhere to watch the Kentucky game?" she asked.

"Exactly," he said. Someone knocked on the door, and they looked at each other in surprise. Molly felt more than a little alarm over the possibility that Cal had returned early and was dropping in on her.

Lately he had become suspicious over the fact that he had never been to her apartment. Reasonably, she wouldn't be able to hold him off much longer on that front, either.

Molly got up to answer and found Mrs. Samperi on the other side of the door. Her eyes were swollen, and she wasn't wearing makeup. Neither Moss nor Molly had ever seen her without. She was one of those people who believed a woman should always "have her face on" and be dressed for the occasion.

"Ma?" Moss said, his tone questioning.

"May I come in?" she asked. She held up her hands. "I promise I didn't bring anything, not even the biscotti Nonna sent for you."

"You can come in," Moss said, his tone wary. His mother was acting strangely. He had never seen her so subdued before. She was usually a livewire, the epicenter of every family function.

"I'll give you two some privacy," Molly offered, turning to go toward her bedroom.

"No, stay," Mrs. Samperi said. "Please, Molly, this concerns you, too."

"All right," Molly agreed, now also wary. She and Moss exchanged a look and he shrugged.

They squeezed together on the couch because it was the only seating in the tiny room. Mrs. Samperi clasped her hands in her lap and cleared her throat. "On the plane ride home yesterday, Joe showed me an interesting video. It was as appalling as you predicted it might be, Mossimo." She paused and sniffed before continuing. "Molly, I am so sorry for the way I treated you. I had no right to show up like that, make unreasonable demands of you, and then hurl insults at you when you wouldn't comply. You are a valued employee, and a treasured member of this family, and I am so very sorry for my behavior. Can you please forgive me?"

"Of course, Mrs. Samperi," Molly said.

"Now, Mossimo," she paused and sniffed again when her voice began to quaver. Molly retrieved a tissue for her. "Thank you, dear," she said, pressing the tissue to her eyes a couple of times before trying again. "Moss, you've always been my baby, my little buddy. You were so easy and so fun that I had a little trouble letting go. I convinced myself you needed me much more than you did, and I set out to make myself invaluable to you. I thought this was for your own good, but really it was for me. I've had a lot of time to reflect on my behavior, and I'm very ashamed. All I ever wanted was to raise a strong man of character, and I've already done that with you. My job is done, and I need to let go. That's not to say that I'm not going to keep interfering in your life because, let's be honest, this is me we're talking about. But I will try to pull it back and keep it to the same level as your other siblings. Will you please forgive me?"

"Ma, of course I do," Moss said, pulling her into a tight hug. "And let's not ignore my responsibility in this. I knew you were babying me too much, and I let it go on because I liked it."

"I love you," Mrs. Samperi said, crying.

"I love you, Ma," Moss said, holding her tightly.

"And we all love Molly," Mrs. Samperi added, opening the hug circle to Molly who also started to cry at being invited into such a tender family moment. In Moss's room, Bella woke from her nap and began to wail.

"Oh," Mrs. Samperi said, mashing her fist to her mouth. "She sounds so much bigger."

"Why don't you get her, Ma? I'm sure she'd like to see her Nonna."

"I'm a Nonna," Mrs. Samperi said, crying all over again, but she slid off the couch and went to retrieve Bella. She was gone a long time, and they could hear Bella laughing, a recent addition to her repertoire of growing milestones. Moss and Molly sat on the couch in silence, both too overwhelmed for words. Eventually Mrs. Samperi returned with Bella.

"She's so beautiful and so content and happy. You two are doing a wonderful job with her," she said. Moss and Molly shared a smile, knowing how much exhausting work had gone into the baby, and appreciating the reassurance. "Now, I'm going to suggest something, and you can say no. But your father is going to watch the Wildcats game today on the big screen, and there will be a lot of food. I thought maybe you could bring Bella and we could have a party."

Moss and Molly looked at each other, trying to tamp down their enthusiasm. "I guess that would be okay," Moss said slowly.

"Good, we'll see you in a little bit," Mrs. Samperi said, heading for the door.

"Uh, Ma, the baby," Moss said when Mrs. Samperi made no move to hand her back.

She looked down, as if surprised to find Bella still in her clasp. "Oh, right. Nonna loves you," she said, kissing the baby's cheeks before handing her to Molly.

They waited until she was in her car and driving down the road before high fiving each other. And then Molly said, "Moss, what video was she talking about?"

Moss froze. "Mol, you really don't want to know. Suffice it to say it's life changing for every Samperi who views it."

"Can't I see it?" she asked.

"Sweetheart, you're living it," he said, and kissed her cheek.

CHAPTER 26

Two weeks before Christmas, Molly walked into the apartment to find Moss sitting on the couch, perfectly still, his hands clasped in his lap. He had asked her to run an errand for him after work, and she had. Now she was exhausted and supper still needed made and the baby fed. To say she was grumpy would be an understatement.

"What are you doing?" she asked.

"Sitting here," he said, making no move to help her with the baby, whose carrier now felt like a bag of cement, thanks to her ever-expanding size.

"Okay," Molly drawled. "Did you make supper?"

"No," he said, shrugging.

"Okay," she repeated. "Is there a reason?"

"I thought we could order pizza," he said.

"Sure," she said, her tone snappish. They had just dropped a hundred dollars on groceries the night before, but far be it for her to once again be the voice of self-restraint. She set Bella down, began unstrapping her, and paused. "What's that sound?"

"What sound?" Moss said.

"It's like a weird swooshing sound," she said. "Don't you hear it?"

He cocked his head, listening. "Oh, that. It's the washing machine."

She had been crouching and she toppled over backwards in surprise. "What?"

Moss couldn't take it anymore. He bounded off the couch and picked her up. "I bought you a washer and dryer for Christmas, and I needed to get you out of the house so I could install them today."

"What?" Molly exclaimed. "Are you serious?"

He led her over to the laundry closet, which to this point had served as a game cupboard and storage area. Inside were a stackable washer and dryer. The washer was running with Bella's laundry inside.

"Moss," Molly breathed. "I cannot believe you did this. But how? How did you afford this?"

"The show got picked up. They haven't even finished putting together the pilot, but they love it. They ordered a whole season and sent us an advance. It was enough to pay for this and the lawyer."

"Moss," she said, jumping into his embrace and hugging his neck. They did a happy dance around the small space while the washer chugged on. "Thank you so, so much. This is amazing. Wait a minute, I'm your secretary. How did I not know this about the show?"

"They called Jess directly and I asked everyone not to say anything so I could surprise you," Moss said.

"There should be a term for this combination of irritation and elation," Molly said.

"There is, it's called being near a Samperi," he said. "Let's order pizza, and not the five dollar special. We're going to get one with everything. No, two so we'll have leftovers. And we're going to get delivery. And this time we won't tip with all the change we can scrounge from the bottom of your purse."

"We're Rockefellers," she said.

"Who?" he asked.

"Never mind." They were giddy as they sat on the couch and poured over which toppings to get and then placed their order. Molly's phone beeped with a text from Cal, but she ignored it.

"What's the problem?" Moss asked.

"No problem," Molly said.

"Mol, I saw your face when the phone beeped. Is something up with you and Cal?"

"You really don't want to hear about it," Molly said.

"If you're having a problem, then I want to know," he said. "What are best friends for?"

"Okay, it actually would help me to have a man's advice," she said.

"Fire away."

"You know I've never…"

He grinned. "I know you've never."

"Well, Cal doesn't. And I've been holding him off, and it's not going over well. I don't know how to keep holding him off without either revealing my secret or crushing his feelings. And I don't want to do either of those things."

He stared at her, blinking and silent.

"You're not saying anything," she said.

"You want me to give you advice on how not to sleep with your boyfriend?" he exclaimed.

"You asked what was wrong; that's what's wrong," she said.

"Dump him," he said.

"What?"

"You heard me. I said dump him," he enunciated the words. "You don't love him."

"We've only been going out a few weeks," she said.

"Molly, why are you being so dumb about this?" he yelled.

"Don't call me dumb," she yelled.

The doorbell rang. "Great, the pizza's here. I hate eating when I'm angry," he said.

"Then don't eat it," she said, snatching the money out of his hand to answer the door. She yanked the door open and saw Cal standing on the other side.

"Hey," he said, smiling.

"Oh," she said, a sinking feeling of dread in the pit of her stomach.

"Oh, hey, it's Cal," Moss yelled, vaulting over the back of the couch to come stand beside Molly. "We were just talking about you."

"What's going on?" Cal asked.

"Nothing. Let's step outside," Molly said. She put her hand on his chest to herd him back outside.

"It's never going to happen, Cal," Moss said, and Molly switched arms to push him inside instead.

"Stop it," she hissed.

"She's never going to sleep with you," Moss yelled before Molly slammed the door in his face.

"What's he doing here?" Cal asked.

"I live here," Moss yelled through the door.

"Shut up," Molly called, banging the door a couple of times with her fist. Inside, Bella began to cry. "Get your child."

"She's your child, too," Moss yelled petulantly before disappearing into the recesses of the apartment to retrieve Bella.

"He doesn't mean that the way you think," Molly explained.

"I have no idea what to think," Cal said.

"Moss is my roommate," she said, and the words hit like an atom bomb.

"Oh," Cal said.

"Strictly my roommate," she clarified.

"That doesn't make it much better," he said.

"I know, it's horrible. I'm sorry, Cal. This all came about when we were first getting together. It was supposed to be temporary, and then it wasn't," she said.

"Molly, I think I've been patient," he said.

"You have," she agreed.

"But I need to see some kind of sign from you that this is going somewhere because right now it feels stuck in neutral. Or maybe even reverse." He paused and scowled at the door.

Molly let out a breath. "Cal, I like you, I really do. I like so many things about you, and I'm attracted to you."

"But not enough," he said.

"But not enough," she said. "I'm so, so sorry. This," she motioned toward the door, "has been kind of a mess. I've tried hard not to let it take over my life, but apparently it has. And I'm so sorry that you got dragged into the mix."

"It's okay," he said. "But, Molly, a word of advice about him from someone who has known him most of my life. Be careful."

"Thank you," she said, stuffing down what she wanted to say, which was that Moss wasn't going to live much longer to inflict more damage. She watched with sadness as Cal turned and walked away. Molly wanted to cry. She had tried hard to be a person of integrity, the kind of person who would never willingly hurt anyone. And she had hurt Cal, in large part due to Moss. She tried to stay outside a while to get control of her anger, but eventually the pizza arrived and she had to go in.

"Oh, good, the pizza's here," Moss said cheerfully, as if nothing had happened. He had doubtless heard her breakup with Cal through the thin door. Knowing him, he had used a glass and pressed his ear to it to eavesdrop.

Molly tossed it onto the kitchen table and headed for her room. "Where are you going?" he said, and she spun on her heel.

"Have you lost your mind?" she asked, and the dam broke on their combined anger.

"Yes, Molly, I have lost my mind. And you know what did it? Seeing you go on date after date with a guy I can't stand, and then hearing you discuss the possibility of losing your virginity to him. Really, how did you think I was going to react to that?"

"I hoped you would be mature enough to give me some advice on how to handle the situation," she said.

"Well, I'm not. But you know what? I don't know many men who would be in that situation," he yelled.

"Keep your voice down," she yelled.

"Make me," he yelled.

"You are such a brat," she yelled.

"And you...*ti amo, e mi stai facendo impazzire,*" he flung his fingers forward in an impassioned Italian gesture, *I love you, and you're driving me crazy.*

"Stop speaking Italian when we're in the middle of an argument. You know I hate that," she said.

"*Perchè pensi che lo faccia?*" he said, *Why do you think I do it?* There was another knock at the door. "I bet it's Cal, come back to lull you to sleep with the pure boredom that radiates from his presence."

"Moss, do not dare get the door," she said.

Smiling as he defied her, he reached for the door and yanked it open.

Bella's mother, Tammy, stood on the other side, a very long and very sharp knife held in her clutched fist.

CHAPTER 27

"Whoa," Moss said, his tone that of someone trying to gentle a runaway horse.

"Give her to me," Tammy said, and she was clearly high beyond all reason.

"Why don't we talk for a while?" Moss said, his voice soothing and gentle. He was standing so close to her and holding Bella in his left arm. One swipe of the knife, and it would be over. Molly edged closer, as silently and slowly as she could so as not to call attention to herself.

"You stole her," Tammy said. "And I need her."

"Why do you need her?" Moss asked.

"Why do you think?" Tammy replied, but Moss and Molly had no idea. Did she want her daughter or did she want to use her in some nefarious purpose for drugs?

"You can have money," Moss said. "Or food or a car or anything you need, but you have to put the knife down."

"Where were you when I was pregnant with her? Where were you when I was in the hospital?" she asked. "It hurt so bad, that was why I started taking drugs again. And it's all your fault."

"I didn't know about her," Moss said. "I would have helped, if I had known."

"I didn't want you to know because I didn't want you to take her, and now you're trying to take her away forever."

"Just until you get some help," Moss said. "Until you're stable. She needs stability."

"Don't you tell me what she needs. She's my baby," Tammy said. She licked her lips, her eyes darting frantically around. Moss used the moment to take a step back, but Tammy noticed and took a step forward.

"Stop moving, or I swear I'll do it," she threatened, gripping the knife closer and waving it back and forth.

"Okay, easy, easy. We can talk, all right? We have pizza. Are you hungry?"

She nodded.

"Let me put the baby down so she'll be safe, and we can talk all you want, okay? I'm sure we can come to some kind of arrangement or understanding," Moss said. He took another step back, and Tammy snapped. Molly had seen too many crazy, out of control people not to recognize the change in her expression. She was close, too close to Moss and Bella. They had no chance. Molly leapt, knocking Tammy backwards so that they both tumbled onto the ground. She didn't feel the knife go in, but she heard Moss's scream, a primal, terrified thing, and she sensed Tammy's fetid panic as she pushed Molly off of her and scrambled away.

"She attacked me," Tammy said. "You saw her attack me."

"No, no, no, don't take the knife out," Moss yelled, but it was too late. With a sickening sliding sensation, the knife came out of Molly's gut.

After that, everything was fuzzy. She thought she heard footsteps, as if Tammy ran away. Bella was crying. Did Tammy have her?

"Bella," she croaked, reaching toward something she could no longer clearly see.

"Bella's safe," Moss said. He was pressing something on her stomach, and it hurt. She wanted to move away from his touch, but she couldn't. He was muttering things and Molly felt warm and sticky and then cold as shock began to set in and she started to shake.

"Molly," she could hear Moss yelling her name, and she wanted to tell him it was all going to be okay. But she couldn't make her voice work, and then her vision started to fade. She was still there, but not there, as the sirens grew nearer. Eventually they came so close the sound began to fill her head, an endless wailing that wouldn't stop. And then it wasn't the sirens; it was Moss. He was screaming her name and, like a switch being flipped, everything turned off and all was silent and black.

For Moss, it was like watching a horror movie in slow motion and fast forward at the same time. He saw Tammy's knife coming toward Bella and he put up his arm to block it, but the arm was knocked away by Molly who, without his notice, had crept close enough to tackle Tammy. For a moment, he had hoped maybe she knocked the knife away. And then, with sickening reality, he saw Tammy pull the knife from Molly's body and plunge it in again and then a third time. He screamed and set Bella in her pack and play. She began to wail, adding to the chaos. With her safe, he could turn his attention to Tammy, but she was already scrambling away in terror, as if she'd had a moment of lucidity and realized what she'd done.

"She attacked me," she said, "You saw her attack me." She reached for the knife again, and Moss yelled. Once on a construction site, one of the workers they occasionally hired when they needed extra help fell from a beam and landed on a broken shard of pipe. Moss had made the call for help, and the dispatcher had told him not to remove the pipe. It went against instinct, but the paramedics had informed him it had probably saved the guy's life. *It needs to be removed at the hospital or he could bleed out,* they had said. And now he was watching as the knife was being pulled from Molly's body, and blood was everywhere, so much blood. Tammy stood and ran off into the night.

Moss's mind was a whirl of panic. He took off his shirt and began using it to try and stop the flow of blood now spurting from Molly's body. How could she survive the loss of so much blood? "Help," he called. "Help me."

A neighbor poked his head out. "What's going on?" he asked, grouchily.

"Call 911," Moss yelled. "Please, she's dying."

He had no idea if the man complied, but he must have because soon sirens and lights were everywhere and they were peeling Moss away from her. The paramedics took over while the police began questioning Moss. "I have to get my daughter," Moss said. The officer followed him into the apartment while he retrieved a wailing Bella and began trying to soothe her.

"Tell me what happened," the officer commanded. "The neighbor said he heard you fighting."

All at once Moss realized they thought he was a suspect. "It was the baby's mother," he blurted. "She's on drugs. She showed up with a knife."

"The baby's mother stabbed your girlfriend," the officer clarified.

Moss nodded. "We're in the middle of a custody case, and I've been trying to find her. She has a drug problem."

"What's her name?" the officer asked.

"Tammy." He paused. He could never remember Tammy's last name. Molly had all the information and usually prompted him. The thought of Molly reminded him of the binders where she kept all their important papers. He reached for one and began sifting until he found a document with Tammy's last name on it. He gave it to the officer.

"Please, can we talk about this at the hospital? I need to be with her," Moss said.

"Do you have someone to help you with the baby?" the officer asked.

"Yes, I need to send a message to my family." The officer took the baby while Moss pulled out his phone and sent a group text. All he could manage to get out was that he and Molly were headed to the hospital and he needed them to come immediately.

"Are you okay to drive or do you want to ride with me?" the officer asked him.

"I'll drive. The car has her seat attachment," Moss said. With shaking hands, he buckled Bella into her carrier and then clicked her into the car.

"Follow me," the officer said.

Moss nodded again, glad to be the recipient of any direction right now. He felt as if he were going into shock himself, but he was glad. He never wanted to replay the last half hour in his brain. For now he was too numb to remember much of what had happened.

He followed the officer to the hospital with no realization of what he was doing or how he got there. The officer stood by while he retrieved Bella's carrier from the car and walked to the emergency room. Joe and Peaches were already there. Moss almost collapsed with relief when he saw them. Joe was the quintessential big brother; he could make everything okay.

"This your brother, Samperi?" the officer asked Joe.

"My youngest," Joe said. "What happened?"

"His girlfriend was stabbed," the officer said.

"Molly?" Joe said, his voice quaking.

"You know her, too?" the officer asked.

"She's our secretary," Joe said.

"I'll come back later," the officer said, his tone suddenly much more sympathetic. Moss realized he had probably still been a suspect, at least in some part of the officer's mind. But the Samperi name carried a lot of weight in the community, and he was thankful to be off the radar.

"Moss, what happened?" Joe said.

Bella began to stir. "The baby. I forgot her bag, and she's probably hungry." He looked helplessly around.

"I'll take the baby," Peaches said. Until this moment, she had never touched or even looked at the baby. A part of Moss's brain noted that it must be an incredibly painful moment for her, but she didn't show it. "Why don't I take her to your place, feed her, and stay with her a while, okay? Then you won't have to worry."

He nodded, mutely handing her the carrier and keys before bending down to hug her. "Thank you. I love you."

"I love you, too. And Molly's strong, she's a fighter. It's going to be okay."

He nodded, but wasn't sure he believed her. She hadn't seen all the blood. "Bella's sleep sack is on the end of her crib, and there's a lion in there. She won't go to sleep without it. The bottles and formula..."

She pressed a hand to his cheek. "Honey, I teach kindergarten. There is literally nothing I can't handle. We'll be fine."

He nodded again. She took the baby and wandered off. "Here," Joe said. He had taken off his hoodie and began putting it on Moss who was still shirtless. Joe was much bigger, and the hoodie hung on him like a tunic. Joe zipped it nonetheless and rolled the sleeves a couple of times, exactly as he had done when Moss was a kid and wanted to wear one of his shirts. "You should wash your hands."

Moss looked at them and realized they were covered with dried blood, Molly's blood.

"Do you need help?" Joe asked, and Moss nodded again. Joe led him into the bathroom and began to gently wash his hands with warm water and soap. The water ran red, then pink, and eventually clear. Joe dried his hands and, with his arm around his shoulders, led him back out of the bathroom again. By that time, the rest of the family had arrived. His mother looked frantic.

"What happened?" she said. "They wouldn't tell us anything."

"Molly was stabbed," Joe said, and there was a general gasp of distress.

"Is she...?" Lou began, her voice breaking. Benny reached for her hand, but he looked none too stable himself.

"We don't know anything yet," Joe said. He led Moss to a chair and bade him sit down. The rest of the family followed suit. The officer returned and gave Moss a statement to fill out.

They waited in silence for what felt like an eternity. Eventually a surgeon emerged in scrubs. "Family of Molly O'Ryan?" he called, and all the Samperis stood up. He paused, taken aback by the sight of so many of them.

"Is there a husband?" he clarified, and Moss stepped forward, not caring at all about the lie. He might legitimately lose his mind if an obscure hospital policy restricting access to family members kept him from Molly.

"Your wife's wounds are very serious, and she's lost a lot of blood. I had to tack up some portion of her bowels, and she's at great risk for infection. We gave her some blood, pretty much all we had on hand. At this point she needs to rest and heal and keep an eye out for infection. If there's no infection, I expect her to make a full recovery. The next twenty four to forty eight hours will tell us a lot."

"Can I see her?" Moss asked.

"Come with me," the man said. Moss followed him to a recovery room where he saw Molly hooked to all manner of beeping machines.

"We had to intubate her for the surgery, but we'll take it out soon. I don't expect a problem with her breathing; it wasn't her lungs that were affected. I know she looks scary now, but most of this will get disconnected after her initial time in recovery."

"Can I stay with her?" Moss asked.

"For as long as you like," the surgeon said.

"Thank you," Moss remembered to say. The man gave him a gentle pat on the shoulder and turned to go. Moss sank into the uncomfortable chair beside the bed, ready for a long night of waiting.

CHAPTER 28

Twelve hours later, they removed Molly's breathing tube. As predicted, she did fine without it. Nurses came in every hour to monitor her vitals, and reported with a smile to Moss that there was no sign of infection.

It was an eventful twenty-four hours, and Moss was anxious to inform Molly when she came to. After the first day, they began dialing back her sedative. She became restless until, all at once, she woke up.

"Why are you wearing a shirt with my name on it?" she croaked to a dozing Moss who startled awake, wondering if he'd been dreaming.

"Because when it came to light that you'd saved my life and Bella's, my mom started saying, 'What would we do without our Molly.' Vivian jokingly said we should put that on a shirt, and Lou had these made up. Everyone is wearing them."

"It says 'Team Molly Samperi,'" she said, squinting.

"Yes, it does," he agreed. "Can I get you anything?"

"A toothbrush," she said, and fell back asleep.

A couple of hours later, she woke again. Moss sat impatiently nearby as a nurse ran through a series of questions and instructions with her. Yes, she was hungry, yes, she could have something to drink, no she couldn't get out of bed yet, yes, they would take the catheter out soon. And, yes, she would help her brush her teeth. She did so, holding a tray beneath Molly's mouth so she could spit into it when the brushing was over.

"Well, that was humiliating," Molly said, but she sounded more like herself, besides the continued scratchiness in her throat.

"Do you need anything else?" Moss asked.

"No," Molly said. She tipped her head to study him. "You're mad at me."

"More than I ever thought possible," he said.

"Because of Cal?"

He rolled his eyes. "Cal's not even a blip on my radar and never has been. I put myself to sleep in this stupid chair thinking of how boring he is. Scientists could study him and sell his body odor as a sedative. I'm mad because you leapt on a woman with a knife. What were you thinking, Molly? How did you see that ending well?"

"I saw it ending well for you and Bella, which was my only concern at the moment," she said.

"Let me tell you something, woman, and hear it well. I am the man in this relationship, and I will do the protecting. So stop it," he said.

"Next time there's a knife-wielding psychopath, it can be your turn to leap," she promised.

"Not next time, all the times," he said. "You almost died, Molly." He finished talking and burst into tears.

"Oh, Moss," she said, wishing she could reach for him, but she was still connected to an IV and pulse-ox monitor. "Could you come here so I can hold you?"

Gingerly, he climbed up beside her in the bed. She put her arms around him, and he rested his head on her chest. "Do you know I've cried three times since I was fourteen, and two of them have been with you?" he said.

She ran her hand soothingly over his head. "How's Bella?"

"Good. My mom, Peaches, and Vivian are taking turns with her. We may never get her back."

"Oh yes, we will," Molly declared, and Moss smiled at her proprietary tone. "Did they find Tammy?"

He tensed. "I was hoping not to have to tell you until later. She borrowed a car from someone. They found it plowed into a tree a few miles from our house that night." He paused. "She didn't make it."

Now it was Molly's turn to cry. "Poor Bella. What are we going to tell her?"

"The truth, the awful, ugly truth," Moss said. They were quiet a few minutes, feeling a mix of grief, relief, and guilt over their relief.

"What a mess," Molly said at last, sniffling. "You, me, Bella, Tammy."

"We are not a mess," he said.

"We're not exactly the Cleavers," she said.

"Who?"

"Never mind."

"I love us," Moss declared. "I love our tiny little apartment and lone, clunky car. I love that we can never find anything to do on a Saturday afternoon, but still end up having fun anyway. I love that you love my daughter so much you literally almost gave your life for her. I love that I'd rather be poor with you than rich with anyone else. I love that your Thanksgiving decorations consist of exactly one four-inch turkey but it still takes you thirty minutes to arrange it. I love that you opened your heart and home and wallet to me when I deserved to be tossed into the street. I love that you've had the patience and skill to teach me everything I need to know to become a functioning adult. I love that you are the first person I see when I wake up and the last person I see when I go to bed. Long story short, Molly O'Ryan, I love you, so, so, so much." He kissed her until the machine that was set to monitor her blood pressure began to beep in alarm.

He pulled away, grinning. "It's nice to see the effect I have on you in black and white."

"You needed proof?" she said.

"No," he said, the old cocky Moss, and she laughed. "I mean, you've been in love with me for three years."

She shook her head.

"No?" he said, sounding slightly less certain.

She shook her head again. "No, I was not in love with you. I was infatuated with you, and I got over it after you took me into the woods and acted like a helpless child."

"What about that kiss, though?" he said. "The one in the woods, the one that went on forever?"

"Oh, no, that kiss was golden. But I wasn't in love with you. In fact, I didn't even like you anymore, if I'm being honest. But I took you in because that's what friends do. And *then* I fell in love with you." She brushed the curls out of his eyes, adoring him with her expression. Moss's heart began to thud painfully and he thought it was a good thing he wasn't hooked up to a blood pressure machine. "Moss, I used to picture the kind of man you might become if you ever grew up, but you crushed that image because you're *so much more*. The way you take care of Bella and me is beyond comprehension. I have never felt so loved or so safe or so much like I belong. I never dreamed I would find the kind of life I've built with you. I spent so much of my life broken, alone, and afraid that I began to wonder if God heard me all those times I prayed. But He did because He gave me something so much more beautiful than I could ever have imagined," she said.

"Dang it, O'Ryan," he said, swiping at tears again. "I have something else to tell you, and I have to get it out before I blubber again."

"Go ahead," she prompted.

"I sold the Love Machine," he said.

"How long was I out?" she asked.

"Long enough for me to contact a guy who has been interested in it for a while. Long enough for my dad to use the money to buy a minivan from a dealer he knows."

She closed her eyes. "Mossimo Samperi in a minivan. No, I can't, the picture won't form," she said.

"How about Mossimo Samperi and family in a minivan," he suggested.

"It's getting clearer," she said.

"There's more," he said.

"I don't know how much more my heart can take, and I mean that literally," she said, glancing at the monitor.

"I asked my parents to let me buy the barn."

"The barn where you grew up?" she breathed, not daring to believe it.

He nodded. "They said no. But they said we could have it for free, as long as we get married first." He plucked a ring box from his pocket and set it on her chest.

"Moss," she said, her tone disbelieving.

"I know it's soon, but I figure we've already kind of experienced our first year together. I mean, we've lived with each other and learned all our annoying habits. And we've spent a sleepless few months with an infant. We've weathered poverty like pros, shared a car, set down a clear division of household duties. To my way of thinking, there's only one thing that's been missing. Hint, hint, wink, wink, nudge, nudge."

"About that," Molly said. "I have a stipulation of my own. I want to wait until our wedding night."

He blinked at her, surprised. "You mean?"

"I mean."

"Wow, you are really going all out in trying to edge out Vivian, Lou, and Peaches for my mom's favorite daughter-in-law. But if that's what you want, then that's what we'll do. It will make a funny story when we tell people you were a virgin when we were married and our daughter was the flower girl at our wedding."

"Thank you," she said, and kissed him. He had to pull away when her alarm began beeping again.

"We're getting married tomorrow, yes?" he said, his breathing lopsided and strained.

"Soon," she said. She kissed him but pulled away again when she began to feel lightheaded. "Very, very soon." Her blinks were growing longer; her eyes felt like cement. "I'm so tired."

"Go to sleep, I'm here for the long haul," Moss said.

"Moss, I love you so," she mumbled groggily, resting her head on his shoulder.

"Molly, I love you more," Moss said. He deposited a gentle kiss on the top of her head and closed his eyes, the sound of her deep, even breathing lulling him into a sleep of his own.

Thank you for reading *A Complete Overhaul,* the third book in The Builders series. For more books, please visit my website at www.vanessagraybartal.com